P. M. Hubbard and The Murder Room

>>> This title is part of The Murder Room, our series dedicated to making available out-of-print or hard-to-find titles by classic crime writers.

Crime fiction has always held up a mirror to society. The Victorians were fascinated by sensational murder and the emerging science of detection; now we are obsessed with the forensic detail of violent death. And no other genre has so captivated and enthralled readers.

Vast troves of classic crime writing have for a long time been unavailable to all but the most dedicated frequenters of second-hand bookshops. The advent of digital publishing means that we are now able to bring you the backlists of a huge range of titles by classic and contemporary crime writers, some of which have been out of print for decades.

From the genteel amateur private eyes of the Golden Age and the femmes fatales of pulp fiction, to the morally ambiguous hard-boiled detectives of mid twentieth-century America and their descendants who walk our twenty-first century streets, The Murder Room has it all. >>>

The Murder Room
Where Criminal Minds Meet

themurderroom.com

P. M. Hubbard (1910–1980)

Praised by critics for his clean prose style, characterization, and the strong sense of place in his novels, Philip Maitland Hubbard was born in Reading, in Berkshire and brought up in Guernsey, in the Channel Islands. He was educated at Oxford, where he won the Newdigate Prize for English verse in 1933. From 1934 until its disbandment in 1947 he served with the Indian Civil service. On his return to England he worked for the British Council, eventually retiring to work as a freelance writer. He contributed to a number of publications, including *Punch*, and wrote 16 novels for adults as well as two children's books. He lived in Dorset and Scotland, and many of his novels draw on his interest in and knowledge of rural pursuits and folk religion.

Flush as May
Picture of Millie
A Hive of Glass
The Holm Oaks
The Tower
The Custom of the Country
Cold Waters
High Tide
The Dancing Man
A Whisper in the Glen
A Rooted Sorrow
A Thirsty Evil
The Graveyard
The Causeway
The Quiet River
Kill Claudio

The Custom of the Country

P. M. Hubbard

An Orion book

Copyright © Caroline Dumonteil, Owain Rhys Phillips and Maria Marcela Appleby Gomez 1968, 2012

The right of P. M. Hubbard to be identified as the author of this work has been asserted in accordance with the Copyright, Designs and Patents Act 1988.

This edition published by
The Orion Publishing Group Ltd
Orion House
5 Upper St Martin's Lane
London WC2H 9EA

An Hachette UK company
A CIP catalogue record for this book is available from the British Library

ISBN 978 1 4719 0063 1

www.orionbooks.co.uk

Karachi, Lahore and Rawalpindi are real cities, as are, indeed, London, Frankfurt and Rome. Gujranwala, Gujrat and Jhelum are real towns between Lahore and Rawalpindi. All the other places in the book are purely imaginary. So are all the people, not least the protagonist. I myself served in the Indian Civil Service in the Western Punjab before Partition, and I paid a visit to West Pakistan not very long after the September War. At neither time were my experiences those of the imaginary Jim Gilruth.

P. M. H.

1

TOBY SAID, "JIM? JIM, I THINK I'VE WANGLED A TRIP abroad for you. That's what you wanted, isn't it?"

I said, "Where to?" I had already in my mind settled on South America. He said, "Pakistan," and my mind abandoned the dream and went to work on the known but buried reality. "That's your old stamping ground, isn't it?" he said.

"It could be. What part?"

"I'm not quite sure. They'll tell you. But I mean —they know you were out there. That's why they got on to you. I said you'd go and see them."

"Who are they?"

There was a pause, and when he spoke his voice was half deflected, as if he was reading from a paper on his desk. He said, "Anglo-Pak Enterprises, they call themselves." He pronounced it Pack. "That doesn't tell us much. I got the impression they were in minerals of some sort, but I'm not sure."

"What do they want, then?"

"A report. A survey on the spot and then a report. Some sort of opinion survey, I gather. Sounding out local opinion on something they're interested in. They assume you have the language and so on. I thought it would be just the thing for you between books. We haven't actually discussed terms, but I've no doubt they'll pay well. I'll deal with them on that, of course. All I want you to do is to go along and see them, and see if it's the sort of thing you could do, and whether you'd like to." For a moment neither of us said anything. Then Toby said, "Jim? What do you think? You'd like it, wouldn't you?"

I said, "Oh, I'll go, all right. It's just— Yes, of course I'd like it. I'm a bit frightened, that's all. It's twenty years, you know, Toby."

"Yes? Well, they know that, of course. So far as they're concerned—"

"No, I wasn't thinking of that. It's me. I've buried it all pretty thoroughly. Of course, I've often thought of digging it up again. But I didn't really think I ever should, and it frightens me, that's all. But I expect in fact I'll get some enjoyment out of it. And you say the money's right."

"I told you, nothing's been said yet. But I assume that. You go and sort out the job with them, and I'll fix the money. Will you do that?"

"All right. Yes, of course. Sorry, Toby. This

must sound all very ungrateful. I should have liked Brazil."

Toby put on his professional desk-side manner. "I know, Jim," he said. "But it's your experience they want, you see. I mean—you don't know Brazil, do you?"

"No, no. All right. I've never sailed the Amazon, I know. And I suppose I never will, as in the song. But don't let it worry you. What's the address?"

He gave me an address in Pump Court and a tele-phone number. "A man called Carruthers. You phone his secretary for an appointment."

"Not my old friend Colonel Carruthers of the Waziristan Scouts? Has he got a stiff upper lip?"

Toby hung back a little. Then he said, "I've only spoken to him on the phone, but I should say his underlip is stiff as hell. Not, I think, the Waziristan Scouts."

"Ah," I said, "one of the Carruthers of Camber-well?"

"Or Coblenz," said Toby. "Anyway, go and see him and tell me what you make of him."

"All right. I will. Sorry to be so irritating."

"That's all right. There's always my ten per cent. But you'll phone at once, won't you? You've got the number?" He repeated it.

"Yes," I said, "I've got it. I'll ring him."

"Right. Good-bye, Jim. Let me know."

"I will. Good-bye, and thank you." Toby swallowed into the receiver and put it down. He was a good agent, and did not have to pretend with me very much.

The first thing I noticed about Mr. Carruthers was his cuffs, or his right cuff, anyway. Almost the whole cuff showed below the coat sleeve, and it was exquisitely laundered. So was his hand, which he held out palm downwards, with the fingers closed and the thumb widely separated, smiling silently into my eyes as he did so. He had the face and head of a jolly monk in a Victorian picture, only there were strands of very dark hair brushed across his tonsure, and I did not think the multitudinous seas would ever, in my mind's eye, wash that white hand wholly clean. He said, "It is nice of you to come along, Mr. Gilruth. Did Mr. Cooper tell you what it is we want?"

I had expected him to say "put you in the picture," just as I expected him to have a reminiscent and superficial knowledge of the country we were there to talk about. I said, "Not really. I gather it's a research-and-report job. That's not primarily my line, you know. I write novels mostly."

He had waved me to a chair and sat down again himself. He sat back in his chair with the desk between us, looking at me with his head slightly on one side. He was still just smiling. "I know," he said. "I have read them. One I liked very much." He waited to see whether I would ask which, but I only nodded, and he went on, "But you have done reports too. I mean, since you left India."

"I write anything I can get paid for," I said.

"That's it. And you know the place we're interested in, and you speak the local language."

"I used to," I said, but he waved this aside.

"It will come back," he said.

"What is the place you're interested in?"

"It's northwest of Rawalpindi, the area surrounding, more or less, a place called Pind Fazl Shah. The civil district is Fazilpur." He pronounced the names with the careful imitative correctness of the radio commentator, and for the first time it occurred to me that he did not know the country himself, but had been scrupulously briefed.

"Yes," I said. "I was at Pind Fazl Shah for a time not long before I came home."

He said, "You were Sub-Divisional Magistrate there in 1945 and 1946." The statement was matter-of-fact and completely neutral. He was not trying either to impress me with the completeness of his information or to convict me of evasion. He smiled slightly as he said it, but he had smiled slightly all along.

I nodded. "That would be it," I said. "What is it you want me to do?"

"We have a development project in hand there. Our people out there will tell you all about it better than I can. My only present concern is to secure your services. Or someone's." He smiled rather more broadly. He was immensely sure of himself and of me. I decided he already knew nearly all there was to know about me, including the color and extent of my bank balance and the rent I paid for Estelle's flat. Such information was said to be available now in business circles. I should have loved to turn him down. He said, "There's a great deal of industrial development now in West Parkistan. I expect you know that."

"I've heard so. I haven't been out there since Independence."

"No. Well, you can understand that in an area like Fazilpur a major industrial development is going to have considerable social repercussions. It is still at present purely agricultural."

"And service," I said. "It's one of the great recruiting grounds, or was in my day. I expect it still is. Half the men have been in the army at one time or another. The cultivation is unirrigated and always uncertain. The pay and pensions come in, rain or no rain." I thought for a moment. "Do the Pakistan Government want their best fighting men drawn off into industry?"

"They want foreign capital."

I nodded. "And you want me to examine the social repercussions of what you propose to do before you do it? That's very considerate of you."

His eyes widened suddenly without changing the expression of his face. I found it rather unnerving. He spoke with an almost finicky deliberation and preciseness. "I think you will find," he said, "that our people out there wish to ascertain local feeling before they commit themselves."

"They want me to ascertain it for them?"

"I think they want an independent view. An independent view still has its value where local interests are heavily engaged. As of course it always did. You know that, Mr. Gilruth. Now—" He sat forward suddenly, and his fierce, jolly face came bobbing towards me over the polished top of his desk. He had finished with handling me, and wanted the whole tiresome business over with. "Now," he said, "can I take it that you'll do this for us? It is expected to take you three weeks or a month. We shall of course pay all your expenses and whatever fee is agreed with your agent on your behalf. Well, Mr. Gilruth?"

He was already half out of his chair, and I as near as nothing said no just to see him sit down again. But I did not really want to say no. The mere trip was a first-class offer, and I had no doubt that Toby was right in thinking he could take them for a reasonably outrageous fee. I got up myself.

"Yes," I said, "all right. I confess I find myself still very much in the dark about what I'm supposed to do. But I expect I'll find out when I get there.

7

Anyway, I think I'd like to go. You'll let Toby
Cooper know the details? I can go any time, more
or less."

Mr. Carruthers said, "I know that," but by that
time I was past caring. He was not the only one
who wanted the interview finished.

I said, "Better get it done before it gets too hot. I
don't know how I'd stand up to June temperatures
after all this time."

"Yes," he said, "I see," but I knew his briefing
had not extended to June temperatures in Fazilpur
and he was no longer interested.

I phoned Toby and told him I had said I was
ready to go but had very little idea what they
wanted. He said, "Does that matter?"

"I suppose not. It's odd, though, isn't it? Why
Coblenz, by the way?"

"Why what?"

"Coblenz. Carruthers of Coblenz. Not Camber-
well, I agree. And certainly not the Waziristan
Scouts."

"Oh, I know. It was the voice, I suppose. I didn't
see him, remember. Does he look English?"

"I don't see why not. But mentally stateless. I
don't think he knows anything about Pakistan but
what he's been told. That's all correct, I don't
doubt. But once he saw he'd got me, he simply
wasn't further interested."

Toby said, "Once we've got the money, nor am

I. I'll get on to them about that and let you know."
He said nothing for a moment. Then he said, "I
can't think why you're making such a thing of it, to
be honest." He sounded mildly exasperated.

"It's a sore spot," I said. "I'm touchy about my
time out there in half a dozen ways, and instead of
talking myself out of it, I've tended to bury it. Now
that I'm being thrown back at it suddenly like this,
I suppose I panic a bit."

"Well, for God's sake, what is there to panic
about? If they don't like what you do for them,
they'll have wasted their money, that's all. No one's
going to review it in the *Times Literary Supple-
ment*."

"I know that. I don't think it's the report I'm
worrying about. Come to that, I still don't know
what that's supposed to be." Toby said nothing, and
I felt him waiting for me to get off the line. "Anyway," I said, "thank you for getting the thing. It's a
godsend financially, I don't mind saying."

"I didn't get it, in fact. It just came out of the
blue. But I'll see the money's right, you can count
on that."

I thanked him and rang off.

Estelle could not see what I was making a fuss
about either. She had thrown her hat and her bag
on to a chair and was standing in front of the long
glass, shaking her hair back out of its professional

formality, when I let myself in. She looked at me out of the glass through the glistening cascade while I told her what had happened. She said, "Good old Toby. I think it's marvelous." She began using her brush. "You won't be very long away, will you?"

"Three weeks to a month, they said. And I don't think good old Toby had much to do with it, though God knows I don't grudge him his cut. These people had decided I was the man they wanted and simply came after me. And not much credit to me, either. It's just that I happen to have been where they want the job done. They're thorough, all right. They know all about my local qualification. Now I come to think of it, they must have started from the other end. But I don't doubt Toby will squeeze a bit more out of them than I could have. That's what an agent's for, after all. Same as a tax accountant. It's always easier to haggle on someone else's behalf, surely."

Estelle stopped brushing and turned and looked at me direct. Her flower-like face could look very uncompromising. She said, "You're an ungrateful bastard sometimes, aren't you, darling?"

"I don't really think it's a question of gratitude or ingratitude. I wouldn't be without Toby for all the tea in China, and I don't say he doesn't do his professional best for me. But he is a professional, after all. As, indeed, I am myself."

She turned and went on with her brushing, only

now she looked at herself in the glass, not me. "I suppose so," she said. She said it very lightly, as though she had no further interest in the subject, but I knew that in fact she was merely dismissing it from the conversation. It was a trick she had that was part of her disconcerting elusiveness. "Anyway," she said, "you'll enjoy it, won't you?"

"I suppose so. It's a thing I've often thought of, of course. To go back for a strictly limited time and with a strictly limited responsibility. It might well lay a ghost or two, at least."

She got up, put her brush down and gave herself a long hard look in the glass. Beauty was her business, and she, too, was every inch a professional. "You have too many ghosts," she said. "It's people you're short on. Are we going out, do you think? I don't want to be late."

We went out, but to a quiet place, and did not talk much. Estelle had something on her mind she did not want to talk about, and I was still disturbed about my projected return to Fazilpur. I had been very young, to my present way of thinking, when I was at Pind Fazl Shah. It was perhaps the only job in my short, not very happy service I had really given my heart to. I had made so many mistakes and so many friends there, and I had been such a much more innocent and incompetent person than I was now. But that was twenty years ago, and I did not know how I should take the thing up again, or

11

which of my successive selves I should, if I went back there, find myself to be. Also, I did not doubt that Pind Fazl Shah, too, had changed, even if it was, as Mr. Carruthers had said, still purely agricultural. If we had both changed almost out of recognition, it could all be fairly easy. But in my experience the past is never so wholly lost, even under the most systematic burying, that you can count on it not to get back at you if the correct stimulus is applied. Few things are more painful than a recrudescence of innocence.

I had begun to worry, too, about the language. I had prided myself on my use of the local Punjabi when I was out there, but I knew that my proficiency had been measured only against the breath-taking linguistic incompetence of the average English official in India. It had been a matter of surprise and compliment then to hear an Englishman talk intelligible Punjabi at all. Now that the Englishman was, as I assumed he was, merely one foreigner among others, I did not see why he should be indulged any more than an Englishman speaking inadequate French in France. And I did not know how my Punjabi, even fully revived, would measure up to this standard.

I went into the flat with Estelle to pick up my things, but did not stay. She said, "I'm tired, Jim" as soon as we got inside. This was a standardized formula of dismissal, but I said, "As a matter of fact,

I'm tired too." She came up and looked at me with more directness and interest than she had the whole evening. She said, "You're worried about this Pakistan thing, aren't you?"

I nodded. "In a way, yes," I said.

She moved away from me, puzzled, but no longer wholly unsympathetic. "I can't understand you," she said. "You've never talked about India much. But it was just a job, wasn't it, like any other job?"

"It was just a job," I said, "but unlike any other job. To me, anyhow. I knew plenty of people who worked at it in the same spirit as they have since worked for trade associations or hardware manufacturers. I need hardly say they were more successful than I was, in India and in industry."

"And didn't bring a load of guilt out of either. But you'd bring a load of guilt out of Dr. Barnardo's. Go on, Jim. I really am tired. Good night."

I kissed her, very chastely, on the forehead and took myself off.

2

TOBY SETTLED WITH MR. CARRUTHERS FOR A FEE OF three hundred guineas, two hundred down and a hundred on completion. He had plainly hoped for more and was disconcerted by his failure to get it, but he concealed his disappointment with his usual professional aplomb. I had, he assured me, carte blanche so far as expenses went. How he thought I was going to live it up, James Bond fashion, in Fazilpur I did not know, but it would not have been fair to ask. They wanted me to go in about ten days' time, and would send me a first-class return ticket to Rawalpindi by B.O.A.C. and Pakistan International Airlines. I was to break my journey at Lahore, where I should be met. At Rawalpindi I should be taken care of by their people on the spot.

I set about my preparations, but apart from getting myself vaccinated and inoculated, there was not in fact much I needed to do. If I was out of Pakistan before the middle of May, I should not have much more to face than the climate of an unimaginably warm and dry English summer. Short of an extra shirt or two, I had the clothes for this. My bank, comforted by the injection of two hundred guineas, gave me some sterling traveler's cheques and some rather greasy Pakistan notes, of unfamiliar design but still, I was glad to find, smelling faintly of curry spices, as the paper currency of Northern India always had if it was not pretty well fresh from the printers. I had never known the explanation of this, but assumed it was something to do with storage conditions in the shops where so much of the currency was held.

I had my first shot at six in the evening and by midnight was thrashing about on my bed, conducting a fierce and interminable argument with no one in particular in a terrible mixture of Urdu and Punjabi, and surfacing occasionally to tell myself that I should be all right in the morning. This, too, was familiar and in its way reassuring. The reaction to typhoid serum is an idiosyncratic business, and I had never been one to take it easily. It was only when my vaccinated arm blew up into throbbing torment that I realized how long I had been away. In the old days I had been vaccinated time and again, often for demonstration purposes in front of the assembled village, and had never expected anything to come of it. Now, like half the population of England, I was no more immune from smallpox than a baby, and I ran all the classic symptoms of primary vaccination.

The point about these trivia is that they sharpened my unwilling sense of time gone, which was at variance with both my emotional urge to see Fazilpur again and my simultaneous shrinking from the prospect. Even physically I was not the same as the person who had left the Punjab in 1947. I forget how often it is that the body is said to renew itself, but twenty years is a fair proportion of anybody's life. When I came to think of it, I saw that no one I met under thirty would have any very effective memory of the old regime at all. If I chose to think of myself as a ghost returning to the scenes of my former preoccupations, I need not expect the new generation to have any more appreciation than the living generally do of what it is that makes a ghost walk. I do not suppose the ghost knows either. He wants to walk, but is not happy doing it, and does not know the reason for either.

The fact that I should find myself in Lahore within a matter of hours after leaving London only sharpened the sense of unreality in which I went about the whole business. That first sea passage to India, all those years ago, had seemed in itself a lifetime, which I remembered as a thing apart, so that the new world I encountered at the end of it felt almost irretrievably removed from the familiar

16

world I had left. To be going back now in the spirit and duration of a bus journey to Edinburgh made it difficult to believe that the place I should arrive at was in fact the same as the place I had arrived at before. Yet my eager fear of it remained, and was only sharpened by the speed and suddenness with which I knew it would be on me. I went about with a torn mind, knowing that I could explain my predicament to no one and should look, at my age and being the person I now was, very silly if I tried.

Estelle made mild fun of my swollen arm, which got in the way of our love-making, but did not harry me with questions or refer directly to our coming separation. There was a curious and unaccustomed tenderness between us during those ten days, which to me was just part of the emotional resurgence of the time. What it was to her I did not know and did not for a moment think to ask. It was as if my old innocence, which I might now be called on to face, had invaded my latter-day relations, hitherto so differently conducted. At least I was grateful for it, and suddenly saw, as I had not when the thing first came up, that I did not at all want to leave her, even for as long as a month. But going I was, in a counted and diminishing number of days, and, if I could only bring myself to believe it, back to Fazilpur.

If the job I was going out to do had taken on a more solid and formidable shape, I might have been less obsessed with the irrational side of my expectations. But I heard and saw nothing more of Mr. Carruthers and was given no further instructions of any sort. Toby salved his professional pride by getting me an advance of a hundred pounds on my expenses. As I had been promised my return ticket and already had as much currency as I thought I could possibly need, I paid this into my bank, and felt myself nearer than I had for some time to being a credit-worthy citizen.

I went to see Toby at his office the day before I left. He was his usual brisk self, but I thought that he too looked at me with a sort of speculative sympathy. I wondered whether I wore my emotional uncertainties very much on my sleeve. I certainly had not mentioned them to him since our first telephone conversation on the subject. He said, "Well, Jim, all set?"

"I think so. I still don't know what I'm being hired for, but if it doesn't worry you, I suppose it needn't worry me."

If he had belonged to an older generation of professionals, he would have leaned back with his elbows on the arms of his chair and his fingertips pressed together. As it was, he leaned forward, thrusting out his handsome jaw and smiling a smile that did not part his lips. He said, "I don't think it need worry you in the least. This is clearly a once-for-all thing, don't you think? There is no question of establishing yourself in the market. Anyhow, I don't doubt that you'll produce an excellent report. I still haven't forgotten the one you did for the solid-fuel people. All about coke stoves and open fires, but I simply couldn't put it down. And this will be much more interesting than coke stoves. Bound to be. I don't mind admitting I expect you to get a novel out of it as well. You'll have it in mind, won't you? I don't expect Mr. Carruthers will read it."

"He's read all of them so far. And liked one, so he said, but he didn't say which, and I didn't ask. But I reckon that was all part of his homework. I imagine that when my name came up, he just sent his glacial blonde out to buy the lot. In paperbacks if possible, but the lot, anyhow. I couldn't help wondering what he'd really thought of them, but I was damned if I was going to ask."

Toby said, "I don't think that matters much, either, do you?" He leaned back. He looked suddenly much younger, with all the cultivated dynamism drained out of him. "I wish you'd stop worrying, Jim," he said. "I don't really know what it is that's worrying you. It's nothing here, is it?"

"Nothing here," I said. "Nothing that's real anywhere, probably. Who was the man who met himself walking in the garden? I think that's what I'm scared of. But ten to one I shan't meet anyone I mind about or even recognize." I got up. "Look

19

after Estelle for me, won't you?" I said.

He said perfectly seriously, "Don't you think Estelle's capable of looking after herself? I do."

"I'm sure you're right. I've taken out an enormous accident policy, by the way. On expenses, of course. If the plane crashes, she'll be quids in."

"Good. I think she'd probably rather it didn't, all the same. You're not on a Boeing, are you? They haven't been very good risks lately."

I shook my head. "A VC-10, according to schedule. 'Bye, Toby."

" 'Bye, Jim. Have a good time."

I left him standing at his desk, still looking at me with that curious speculative unease. I decided I needed a drink, and went after one.

At about two o'clock on the morning I left, Estelle said suddenly, "Jim? Jim, are you still awake?"

I turned over and put out a hand to her. "Yes," I said. "I didn't know you were. Why are you? You won't look right tomorrow if you don't sleep."

"Jim—you will come back, will you?" She said will you, not won't you. It was not an appeal, not even a sentimental gesture. It was a genuine inquiry, and I wondered what had put it into her head.

I said, "I suppose so. I still find it difficult to persuade myself that I'm even going. I hadn't thought about coming back. But—I assume so, of course. What makes you ask?"

She rolled over and turned her back on me. "I don't know. I wondered, that's all. Now I'm going to sleep. You don't have to be up specially early, do you?"

"No," I said, "plenty of time."

She said "Mm" into the pillow, and a minute or two later quite certainly was asleep. I myself was so certain I should not sleep that I stopped worrying about it, and must have gone to sleep quite soon afterwards. But it was poor sleep. I woke with full daylight on my eyes, and found Estelle already up. The flat was completely quiet against the perpetual background of traffic noises. I thought, "She's gone," and sat up sharply in the bed. Then the door of the bathroom opened and she came out in her dressing gown.

There is something extraordinarily touching about a modern woman stripped of her make-up and with her hair brushed out loose. She faces a man with a half-defensive, half-defiant look in her eye, daring him to love her less for it. In the hearty, athletic period of English history they used to say of a man that he peeled well, meaning that he looked well with his clothes off. The woman nowadays who peels well is the one who looks well with her make-up off. The mere removal of her clothes is nothing to it. Estelle peeled very well indeed; and yet I should no more have thought of asking her to go about like that than I should of asking her to go about naked. She came and sat on the edge of the bed, and we looked at each other in the pale early-morning sunlight. The floor of my whole world moved under me, and I did not know what was going to happen to me at all.

She said, "I had to get up, or I shall be late. You said you had plenty of time, so I didn't wake you. You looked very tired. Didn't you sleep well?"

"Not very well, I don't think. I thought you'd gone."

She shook her head, never taking her eyes off me. "You're the one that's going," she said. "Today. Don't you remember?"

"I suppose so. I'd better be getting up." I put out my hand and touched her arm below the short sleeve of her dressing gown. It was very much a young woman's arm. Too young. I sometimes wondered why she bothered with me. She did not move at all. She just sat there and looked at me, letting me run my fingers up and down the cool skin. "I don't want to go," I said.

"No, but you must, mustn't you? You've taken the plunge. You're in the stream. Anyhow, it will be very good for you."

"Me or my work?"

"Well—both. I know you're not a Significant Figure in Contemporary Literature"—she made the capitals audible—"but it's your job, and you may as well get on with it."

"What about you?"

"I don't know. But there's no harm in finding out." She got up from the bed and went over to her dressing table. She dressed, as she did everything else in relation to her body, with a sort of serious deliberation. I had watched her so often. But this morning I got up, feeling blowsy and rather hollow, and went across to the bathroom. When I came out she was dressed and making coffee in the kitchen. I drank a cup of coffee with her. It was all the break-fast she ever had. It was all I wanted myself this morning. I had no stomach for food, and in any case everyone said that these long flights were a practically non-stop eating marathon.

"I must be going," she said. "Have you got much to do?"

"No, no. Just pick my stuff up and lock the flat. I'm all packed. And weighed to the last ounce. I don't know why when I could no doubt charge up excess baggage to expenses. But it probably cut out a lot of stuff I'll never need, anyway."

We stood in the doorway facing each other. I was never allowed to kiss her when she was made up for work. We just touched fingers. She said, "Good-bye, Jim. Have a good time."

"You too," I said.

After she had gone I washed up the coffee things and put them away. I did not want her to have to wash my cup when she came back from work.

23

When I let myself into my flat, I did not at all like the look of it. Suitcase, briefcase, typewriter, all ready and labeled. I was all set to be the interesting international traveler, marching keenly up the gangway to smile at the air-hostesses clustered in the doorway of the plane. The whole thing ought to have been exhilarating, and I added to my burden by feeling guilty that I was not enjoying it.

The big international airlines have so far just about kept their heads above the rising tide of cynicism and indifference, and are where the railways were, I suppose, a hundred years ago. Romance, unseen or otherwise, no longer brings up the nine-fifteen, but people who are not traveling go to London Airport because the place excites them. It must be a long time since anyone was excited by Waterloo Station. We all know, as the Victorians did not, what it is to cover the ground at seventy miles an hour. We can do it ourselves, and only have to go on doing it long enough to get to Penzance or Inverness or somewhere else in the middle distance. But we cannot, on our own, fly at thirty-five thousand feet and come down at Buenos Aires or Bangkok, and if a man can do it with a proper aplomb and take us with him, we do not grudge him his gold braid and an air of aloofness. By the time I had checked in and was awaiting my call I was consciously acting the habitual traveler. When, herded into our ridiculous airport bus, we were trundled up to what was palpably a Boeing and not a VC-10, I even achieved a momentary shadow of actual physical apprehension. With any luck, now, I should enjoy myself at least as far as Karachi. Beyond Karachi I would not for the moment look. As Estelle had said, I was in the stream, and I could let it carry me until the banks began to look dangerously familiar. Like most Punjabis, I had never known Karachi in the old days, except as a name in another Province; and the other Provinces had been as remote and foreign to us as Italy to a Scandinavian.

There was only a handful of passengers starscattered over that monstrous vista of scientifically designed seating. It was like paying the top price to see a not very popular film. I spread myself over the three seats placed at my disposal and took refuge in an unexpected amusement. We came down, or so we were told, at Frankfurt and Rome. The German plumbing was better than the English, the Italian not so good. The only intimation of a foreign culture was the unexpected attendance of tremendous white-uniformed German women in the men's lavatory at Frankfurt. Clock time fell away in huge uneven chunks and darkness surprisingly kept pace with it. Whenever we had left London, it was undeniably two in the morning when they opened the doors of the plane at Karachi; and then, after twenty years, I suddenly smelled the East.

3

IT TOOK ME A LITTLE TIME TO ACCEPT THE FACT THAT I was a foreigner in a foreign country. I felt so much the returned wanderer that the remote, watchful faces of the immigration and customs men seemed even a little absurd. But my passport said only that I was British and a writer, and we all talked careful official English. I discovered later that the word foreigner had acquired distinct overtones in Pakistan. To say a man was foreign meant that he was white, rather as in England to say a man was an immigrant meant that he was colored. If he was an Indonesian, or an Arab, or even an Indian, they said so. If he was French or German or English, he was foreign. I still do not know whether this was the instinctive defensive nationalism that made nineteenth-century China call all Europeans foreign devils, or whether it was a leftover from the old imperial days when all mankind had been divided, for certain purposes, into Indians and Europeans. Whatever it was, I was a foreigner, and was received with the proper cautious courtesy, at least until I began talking Urdu.

The night was sultry, as it never is in the Punjab until much later in the year. Once discharged of the official procedures, I walked out into a familiar timeless world. Muffled figures slept on steps and benches. It was not, as at home, questionable merely to be abroad, but all action was suspended. I told the taxi driver where I was scheduled to spend the next five hours. He woke himself up heaving my suitcase into the boot, and when we were under way said, "You're not a Pakistani, are you?"

"I'm English," I said. It seemed odd to have to explain this.

"But you speak Urdu." He was puzzled, even mildly indignant.

"I was working here in the old days."

"What sort of work were you doing then?"

"Government work."

"Before Partition?" He used the English word, and another small piece of the unfamiliar picture slipped into place. To Pakistan, 1947 was, above all, Partition. All the other old imperial provinces, from the United States downwards, celebrated Independence, but the Pakistani celebrated his separation from India. Independence, of course, went with it, but it was the separation his mind seized on.

I said, "That's right, and he grunted. He was quite a young taxi driver. The fact that I, who was now a foreigner, had once been a government man meant nothing to him. He said, "Have you got any pounds you haven't declared?"

"One," I said. "Why?"

"I'll give you fifteen rupees for it. The banks give you thirteen."

"But why do you want it?"

"I want to buy something."

I did not question the logic of this. To find my shaky native sterling thought of as a hard currency, to be bought surreptitiously in taxis, was an unexpected reassurance. "All right," I said, "if it means so much to you." I had brought in my smuggled currency inadvertently, in the hip pocket of my trousers. I gave him the limp green note, and he passed over the spicy local paper, driving fast over the uneven road with his spare hand. We parted with tremendous cordiality. I assumed something was wrong, and found later that I could have got twenty rupees for my pound almost anywhere.

The room had the familiar height and bareness, but there was a shower cabinet in one corner and an unfamiliar air-conditioning unit worked into the lower half of the window. The bearer was an older man, like all the bearers I had ever known, and we slipped at once into the old, slightly solemn professional relationship. He suggested tea, and later, when I was in the shower, I heard him coughing discreetly outside the door, to avoid the intolerable embarrassment of finding me with no clothes on. I came out with a towel around my waist. I sat on the edge of the bed, with the ceiling fan turning very slowly over me, while he pottered about, shaking out and folding the creased and rather sweaty clothes I had traveled in.

I remembered now—how well I remembered—that in this country you were never alone. If you wanted solitude, you asked for it, or at least contrived deliberately to secure it. Then the contrivance affected the quality of the solitude, and you were conscious all the time of eyes obediently or politely averted and ears listening within earshot. I sipped the disembodied tea and the only too full-bodied milk, and watched the old man trying, with a sort of dignified despair, to think of something to do to justify his continued presence. Finally I said, "I've got to go on to Lahore."

He stopped trying to do anything, and stood there with his hands hanging. "That's right," he said. "The bus leaves at half past seven."

"Good," I said. I put down my teacup with a decisive clink. "Can you call me at seven?"

"Seven. Very good. Shall I take the tea things?"

"Yes, take them." He took up the tray with a sort of eager relief and then, with his hands once more occupied, stood there looking at me. "You've been here before?" he said.

"Yes." This was going to be a regular gambit, and I might as well get it right. "Yes, but that was twenty years ago. I was in government service before Partition. Not here. In the Punjab."

"You speak Urdu." He wanted, with the courtesy which was instinctive to him, to explain what might have seemed an intrusive question.

"I used to," I said. "I have forgotten. It will come back, I hope."

"No, no. You speak it very well."

This was not at the moment true, but he said it less from a desire to please than from his own pleasure at finding a foreigner talking intelligibly at all. I shook my head and said again, "It will come back gradually, I hope. Now I must rest for a bit."

"That's right. You rest." We exchanged formalities, and he got himself out of the door, which he shut quietly but very firmly behind him. I turned out the bedside light and lay back, arranging the sheet carefully over my stomach under the gentle down-draft of the fan. I was back, all right. Already the country was pressing in on me, as it always had. But I'm virtually a tourist, I told myself, a visitor. Whatever the country is waiting for, it is not waiting for any decision of mine. I am no longer responsible for anything. But the old disquiet was there, and I did not sleep during what was left of the night.

Morning came with a soft air outside and the phrenetic twittering of hundreds of small birds. They scuttered about in the flowering trees of the compound, where the all-night lamps looked hot against the spreading grey. They did not sing or fly, but dashed about in the branches, working themselves up into a tizzy. Somewhere to the south, only a taxi ride away, there must be the sea, and I was about to put myself the best part of a thousand miles away from it. That had always been a part of the horror, the feeling of being landlocked, so that the infinitely remote sea became not only the escape route but an end in itself.

> *Hence, in a season of calm weather,*
> *Though inland far we be,*
> *Our souls have sight of that immortal sea*
> *That brought us hither.*

I used to read that with the Punjab plain all around me in the motionless aridity of the hot weather. Even now I find it full of an almost physical longing that has nothing to do with intimations of immortality. I washed and shaved and packed my suitcase firmly before the old man brought my tea and could get his hands on it. Apart from dozing a bit on the plane, I had not slept since I left London at midday the day before: but I did not know how long ago this was. I felt a little light-headed and full of a consciously unreasonable apprehension.

31

Pakistan International Airways had Trident jets and bright young air-hostesses. The passengers included purdah women in all-enveloping *burqas* and one venerable figure with a hennaed beard and a green turban who looked as if he had just got back from the Haj by camel. The old man buckled his seat belt around his embroidered coat and sat back with dignity and composure. He looked perfectly in place. It was the hostesses who looked irretrievably in fancy dress. The man next to me said, "Going to Lahore?"

His English was so good that it extended even to the traditional English mispronunciation of the name, which turns the open A into a neutral vowel. He had a clipped toothbrush mustache and a cheerful smile.

"For the moment," I said, "yes. I'm going further up later."

He nodded. "Going up to Pindi, eh? Going straight through to Pindi myself. Been posted." He used an almost perfect version of the Camberley dialect.

I said, "You're army, I take it?" It was purely a conversational link. If he had been wearing battle dress with regimental flashes the question could not have been more unnecessary.

"That's right," he said. "You in business?"

"Well—not really. I'm a writer. But I've come out on a particular job. I was a government servant out

THE CUSTOM OF THE COUNTRY

here, as a matter of fact, before Partition."

I wondered as I said it why I felt compelled to tell him this. It was not part of the standard gambit. There was no more question of my talking Urdu to him than there was of my telling him he spoke English well. But I wanted people to know, as if I was claiming a sort of second citizenship. There had been, in the old days, this passionate dislike of the tourist, the person who had merely come to see the country, and who for this reason saw so much more of it than we did. I belonged, even if I belonged to a country that no longer existed, and I wanted people to know it.

He looked straight ahead, still smiling. He said, "So you must know the place a bit, eh? You'll find a lot of changes."

"Yes, I'm sure. I'm looking forward to it tremendously." This was not entirely true, but it served. He had meant, of course, changes for the better. Everything on the move since the dead hand had been lifted. I was not going to be burdened with that. The thing to do was to throw up my hands in admiration and keep my reservations visibly to myself. I had in fact downwinded him for the moment, and he did not say anything. He still smiled. I said, "I'm surprised to find so much English everywhere. I had expected there to be less. To what extent is it used in the army?"

"It's the language of instruction and communication for officers. With the *jawans*, of course, we use Urdu."

He spoke a little stiffly, and I did not press the point. I said, "Did you see anything of the recent fighting?" and he beamed at once.

"I myself," he said, "unfortunately very little. But it was a wonderful show. A pity it didn't last longer, really. Seventeen days is not enough."

"Enough for what?"

"To weed out the men at the top. It always needs doing, you know. But it was a wonderful show. We gave the Indians a shake-up, I can tell you. And the Yanks."

"The Americans?"

"The Americans, by God. They were behind it, you know. I tell you, American generals in Indian G.H.Q. all through the action. We had intelligence reports. I tell you, they didn't know what had hit them."

I said mildly, "I hadn't thought of your September war as a sort of Bay of Pigs, I must say." I think he must have missed this. He was looking out of his window, still smiling. I leaned slightly across him and looked down. The vast yellow country looked as inhospitable as the mountains of the moon. "But it couldn't go on, surely," I said. "There'd been pretty heavy losses, hadn't there? Material, especially."

"They couldn't go on," he said. "They were

counting on a quick break-through to Lahore. When we held them, they had to pull out."

I did not want to dispute this. Come to that, it was probably true—as true as any rationalization of any war ever is. I said, "There's no question which side public opinion was on at home, at any rate."

He did not respond to this at first. After a bit he said, "You mean on our side? Why was that, do you think?"

"I think two reasons mainly, even apart from Kashmir. Neither of them very good, perhaps. But public opinion seldom is very reasonable. One reason was simply that one always tends to back the smaller man against the bigger. But mainly we weren't sorry to see India burn its fingers in a public act of aggression after years of public righteousness. They'd got away with Goa, more or less. They got away with Hyderabad completely. We didn't want them to get away with this. I suppose we were getting our own back for Suez. Not very noble, of course. But for what it was worth, the sympathy was all on your side."

He turned and looked at me. He was still smiling, but his lips were pursed tightly under his bristling mustache. He said, "Sympathy's all very well, my friend. The Indonesians sent us arms. You stopped sending them."

"I can see that. We stopped sending them to both sides, of course."

He looked out of the window again. "They had plenty already," he said.

"But you held them," I said, and he cheered up at once.

"We held them," he said. "I tell you, a wonderful show."

They served us an elegant breakfast, all put up on a plastic tray in little polythene bags in the best airline style—me, my Sandhurst-speaking companion, the venerable Haji, the purdah ladies and the family two rows back with the gaggle of noisy children, who looked as if they had come straight out of the back streets of a small town with open drains and mangy dogs asleep on the brick paving. This was something totally new. Not my being there with them, because I was at best a ghost, but their being all there together. There was a strong and unfamiliar whiff of democracy in it. A democracy, I supposed, of new money. They had all paid their fares. And of course we all ate the same breakfast, with no communal taboos to complicate the service. I faced for the first time the fact that the Lahore we were all descending on was a Lahore with no Hindus or Sikhs in it. Life was presumably that much simpler, however appalling the process of simplification had been.

I chatted desultorily with the Major—I did not of course know that he was a major, but that seemed about right—at intervals during the rest of the flight. He showed no further interest in my previous experience of the country, and we kept off the recent war. He was not, heaven knows, the first man I had met who saw a wonderful show in a fight he had taken no part in; and I had no reason to think that if the draw had been different he would not have flung himself against the Indian armor with the same heedless gallantry as his fellows, and with the same result. It was only his style that was against him, and that was as harmless as any other professional trick. There could, after all, be no harm, only a profound oddity, in borrowing the English ruling-class voice in a country the English no longer ruled. He pointed out that the orange on the breakfast tray had the thin, loose-fitting skin of the old Punjab fruit over the body of a perfect Spaniard. A new variety, he said, they had evolved a year or two back. It was the only recent achievement of his country available for immediate demonstration, and he demonstrated it with a single-minded enthusiasm.

I tried to recognize the Lahore swinging in great arcs underneath us and glimpsed at intervals across the Major's sharply cut tweeds, but I could make nothing of it. By the time we came down there was nothing to see except dusty tarmac and the huddle of airport buildings. All airports are flat, but here the whole world was flat. The cloudless bowl of pale blue sky ran down everywhere to meet the dust haze on the horizon, and nothing broke the line. This was the great plain that had scared the life out of me before and would no doubt, given the chance, do the same again. Only this time it would not have the chance. I did not know how long I was expected to stay in Lahore, but Fazilpur was a different world.

I said good-bye to the Major, who wished me a pleasant trip. We filtered down the gangway with our hand baggage and straggled across the tarmac through the hard, unwavering sun heat towards the waiting shadow of the buildings. There was a good deal of shouting in the echoing hall. The noises were all much more familiar here. I collected my suitcase, refused a porter, mainly because he spoke to me in English, and went out into the reception space with my hands full. A small pale man came up to me and said, "Good morning, Mr. Gilruth. I have a car here. Will you come this way?"

I nodded, this being the best I could do without putting something down. "Good morning," I said. "Lead on."

4

TO TELL THE TRUTH, I HAD NEVER MYSELF BEEN MUCH of a one for Lahore. It had been the social and official center of our world, except for those of us who went into the Government of India and got sucked into the Delhi-Simla syndrome. There were always the Lahore sort of people, but I was never one of them. Looking back, I think I must have been a difficult young man for any official hierarchy to digest. I had something of a contempt for conformity but a deficiency of any real capacity for effective independent action. The first prevented me from being one of the Lahore people and the second from making good in the comparative autonomy of the districts. The fact that I was in the wrong job did not prevent me from taking it pretty seriously. I believed, and was of course encouraged to believe, in the great Punjab Commission myth, and was too

simple to see that it had receded into the realms of
the purely mythological long before I was posted
to the Punjab. My time out there was, if you like to
put it like that, a formative experience, but it was
not happy.

I was never stationed in Lahore. I admired and
despised the Lahore people, and almost from the
start mistrusted them. It was probably only the mis-
trust that was justified. At any rate, Lahore remained for me a sort of unholy promised land, rich
in slightly sour grapes. I returned to it now rather
in the spirit of a poor relation visiting the family
seat after an agrarian revolution had put the tenants
in possession. The small pale man got into the front
seat beside the driver, leaving me in the back. The
driver wore a peaked cap and a limp khaki jacket,
like a chauffeur in undress uniform. We none of us
said anything, and I watched Lahore unroll itself,
from the cantonment, through the civil-lines area to
the main shopping center of the Mall. Places I
thought I knew but could not be sure of, places I
certainly knew but could not square with my
memory of them, places that were immediately
identifiable. The hotel was, superficially at least,
completely unchanged.

We all got out and the driver handed my things
over to the hotel servants. The small man said, "You
are booked in here, Mr. Gilruth. There is a room for
you. Please order anything you want."

40

"Right," I said, "thank you. Do you know how long I shall be staying here?"

"I do not know that. But you are to make yourself comfortable, please. When you are settled, someone will come and see you. Mr. Aziz, I think. But there is no hurry for that. You will want to look around, I expect. There are always taxis available here."

I thanked him again and we shook hands. Then he got in beside the driver and the car moved off. I never knew his name or, now I come to think of it, his nationality. It was all a bit odd, but on the face of it I had really nothing to complain of.

My rooms confirmed my impression that the hotel had not changed noticeably in the last twenty years. It had, I supposed, been dusted occasionally in the interval, but not to any great purpose. The effect was drab and stuffy. Twenty years ago the bathroom, with piped hot and cold water and flush sanitation, had seemed civilized to a man in from the districts and used to commodes and tin tubs filled from a goatskin bag. Now it lacked glamour. The taps had dripped so long that the stains on the enamel would have been ineradicable even if anyone had tried to eradicate them. The water closet worked, but the seat was cracked and the bowl had the clinging, stale smell of an apparatus that was never properly cleaned. The tiled floor was patched and uneven and the towels disturbingly off-white. I

41

remembered Toby urging me to enjoy myself on expenses, and wondered what James Bond would have made of it. From the back, where the bedroom and bathroom had skylights high in the wall but no windows, there came a constant muted clamor of local voices, as if there was a debating society in continuous session in the dusty sunlight outside. It was all frighteningly familiar.

The odd thing was that what I experienced was not my wary resignation of twenty years ago, but something very like the desperation of my first arrival in the country. Yet this was nonsense. What had frightened me then had been the consciousness of unqualified responsibility in and for an alien and overpowering world. Now I could not bring myself to believe I had many real responsibilities, and I was on the face of it reasonably well qualified to deal with any that might appear. But a touch of desperation was there. I think the truth is that I had buried the past so securely that I had buried my defenses along with it, and the place, simply as a place, affected me almost as if I was meeting it for the first time.

I sent my travel-stained clothes to the wash, put on something more suitable and walked out, still light-headed for lack of sleep, to revisit Lahore. It was already surprisingly hot—much hotter, as I remembered, than it should have been at that time of the year. Lahore was a bedlam, apparently prosperous, certainly cheerful, but a bedlam. There was a steady background of mechanical noise from building operations, but mainly it was the cars, everything from big American limousines to two-stroke three-wheeler rickshaws, driven madly in all directions as fast as their mechanical condition would allow. They all hooted all the time. The drivers had one hand on the wheel and the other on the horn button. They hooted even when they were stopped. The voices of electric horns, some staccato, some long-drawn, rose from all over the town, like the voices of sheep on the move in an English valley. The dust, which as I remembered it had risen only for the occasional disturbance, now hung in the air all the time. It still smelled the same, with an added dash of exhaust fumes, and lodged wherever it could get a hold.

They were building everywhere, government buildings, hotels, office blocks, all of them faced with fretwork panels roughly molded in concrete. The scaffolding looked improvised and uncertain. There was a constant hammering above the grinding of the concrete mixers, as if the builders were laboring to put a hand finish on the elaborate designs roughed out by their wooden molds. Even where they were not building they said they were going to. Every open space that had once been a garden, or at least a bit of grass and trees with its runnels of canal water, now had a notice saying that it was the site for a girls' school, or a Muslim League office, or an agricultural research center. The notices were in English. The promise was still, as it always had been, very nearly as good as the performance. Once the notice was up you had done your best, and the schoolgirls or the Leaguers or the agricultural chemists could be expected to wait with proper patience until the money was available or the materials released and the actual building could begin. But this was for the future. In the meantime your intention was there, publicly stated in English. Some of the notices looked as if they had been there a long time, and the paint was starting to go.

The old queen no longer sat crossly under her elaborate marble canopy. The canopy itself, beautifully finished in the rococo Islamic favored by the imperial designers, stood in the middle of its grass plot, and the students sat under it reading shoddy little textbooks with the remembered air of casual desperation. Further along the Mall, Lawrence, in his soft top boots, no longer offered Lahore the choice between pen and sword. The inscription had gone even in my day, and now Lawrence and his offending symbols had gone too. Kim's Gun had been moved to a traffic island and surrounded with flowers at the expense of some firm who took credit publicly for their public spirit. The gun had, as far as I could remember, a respectable history before the British, or even the Sikhs, got their hands on it.

Only a former vice-chancellor of the university, undeniably English but innocent of any political taint, still faced the traffic in his bronze academic robes. The beggars, surely the same beggars surprisingly little aged, still paraded their deformities in the few places where the cars could not get at them. The edges of pavements broke off short in standing pools of dust, and there was orange peel, whether of the improved or unimproved variety, thick underfoot. Everyone, except for professional reasons the beggars, was immensely cheerful.

And there was new money everywhere. New men in new cars and new clothes, spending money in new shops and restaurants. The old Hindu stranglehold on business had vanished without trace, and the Pakistan rupee, whether or not it was soft even against sterling, seemed to be circulatig very briskly in the hands of its new owners. The place had the garish ebullience of nineteenth-century England, but fewer inhibitions. The cinema posters, still handpainted in a lively pop-art tradition, concentrated on sex with all the single-mindedness of their Western counterparts. The great bodies were clothed from neck to ankle, but the shining draperies clung close to the seductive curves, and the nipples of the tremendous breasts were elaborately highlighted. The Islamic state had thrown up, at least in Lahore, a curiously materialist and secularist society. Compared with the sedate and well-trimmed provincial capital I remembered, it was as if a Butlin's holiday camp had been put down in the cathedral close at Barchester. It was simply a matter of which you preferred.

I drifted through the dusty babel, more of a ghost than ever, but more than ever uncertain what it was I had come to haunt or why. The hotel seemed quiet when I got back to it. The roar of traffic on the Mall was faint here, but the horns still bleated continuously all around the sky. Once they were on your mind, you heard them all the time. The voices at the back went on with their interminable conversations. I imagined the string beds clustered half in the shade, with the bedding rolled up in a bundle at one end. There were figures, some sitting, some lying back with one knee drawn up. There would be a hookah or two, but from where I was I could not hear the long throaty bubble as the smokers drew on them. I could not hear what was said, bar a phrase or two and the familiar conversational gambits. I tried anxiously to decide whether I could follow the drift of English conversation similarly filtered and told myself I could not.

The hotel food was awful. I felt more certain than ever that James Bond would not have liked it. For him, of course, there would have been the wonderfully self-contained dark girl with the sports car out in front and a single table near the door. There was in fact a woman in Pakistani clothes sitting by herself. She was beautiful, but I did not for a moment suppose she was for me. There had been in the old days a tremendous built-in hoodoo against finding the women of the country attractive. It was part of the service ethos, inherited from the dedicated and probably mother-dominated Victorian pioneers who had replaced the easy-going exploiters of earlier times and made the Punjab what it had been and was still, in my day, supposed to be. It was the understood thing that you waited for the English girls who came out in a steady stream to meet your requirements. But in those starchier days they mostly expected marriage as a pre-condition to any pleasant indulgences. It was marriage they came out for. If you wanted casual excitement and were posted anywhere where it was to be had, you could try the Anglo-Indian girls, who at least wore European clothes. I had never made love to a woman wearing the local dress and wondered how you set about it. I had tried rape cases, where the pajama trousers with the string brutally broken were a standard part of the evidence. The defense invariably alleged that it had been broken *ex post facto* by the complainant's brother in defense of the family honor, and no doubt the defense was very often right. I supposed in a case of seduction you merely untied it, or asked her to do it for you. The speculation intrigued me, and I seemed further than ever from the old oppression which I had come back to outface if I could.

Meanwhile the woman in Pakistani clothes sat there by herself, very dignified and composed. The servants buzzed around her in deferential excitement, and I caught snatches of a charming, throaty voice, but could not hear what she was saying to them.

For dinner we abandoned the ordinary dining room and ate in what was called the grill room. This had been vamped up into a dreadful version of Western modernity, and there was a dance band with a man singing. They were all Pakistanis, and played their Western instruments and sang their English words with a solemnly determined gaiety that I found at first extraordinarily sad and then, as it went on longer and got louder, almost intolerably harassing. We were a mixed company: foreign families staying in the hotel; visiting businessmen of every sort of nationality, often dining with Pakistani hosts; Pakistanis in twos and threes out on the town for an evening's high living. I did not see my solitary beauty anywhere. The food was more ambitious but equally unsuccessful. I was very tired and the noise was giving me a headache. I ate what seemed best and went to my room.

Wherever your room was, you got to it by walking through the hotel compound. All the rooms were self-contained suites—bedroom, sitting room and bathroom—with a single door opening on to the compound. When I came to think of it, it was a sort of early version of the motel. People, in fact, had

their cars parked in front of their rooms. There was
no hotel corridor with its dressing-gowned figures
diving furtively in and out of labeled doors. Bedroom farce here would be at least partly an outdoor
sport. It was quite dark, and cool now. The stars
were the familiar English stars, but riding unnatu-
rally high in the sky, so that Orion's head brushed
the zenith and Sirius blazed over the hotel roof.
There had been water run through the garden wa-
tercourses. The smell of sodden earth was stronger
and more reminiscent than the smell of the flowering trees, but I had no heart for the too familiar
night.

The room felt hot and stuffy after the freshness
outside. I undressed and turned the fan on gently. I
was dead tired but unwilling simply to go to bed.
There was a local newspaper, printed in English, on
the table. It must have been supplied by the hotel
as required reading for foreign visitors, and I took it
up. The Foreign Minister had made a speech warn-
ing all enemies of Pakistan that she had the will and
the power to resist aggression. The Governor of
West Pakistan had made a speech saying that only
by maintaining the Islamic ideals and reviving the
spirit of social service could the Pakistanis build a
prosperous state. The President had said that unity
was strength, and that any threat to the essential
unity of Pakistan was a threat to the very life of the
nation. All three were reported at tremendous length

with photographs. A small news paragraph on the front page said that three local leaders in what used to be Bengal had been arrested for advocating a measure of independence for East Pakistan. There was some sports news, a financial page of surprising sophistication and a sprinkling of heavily slanted foreign news. About the only home news was the report of a case in which a foreign woman alleged rape by Pakistanis in one of the suburbs. I read it all carefully.

When I got to bed the conversations outside had stopped, and after a bit I slept. I do not know what time it was when the dog began crying at the back. The cries gradually penetrated my sleep. They were a succession of long and desperate whimpers, almost small screams, forcing themselves regularly out of the anguished body. No one was torturing the dog. No one was taking any notice of it at all. I pictured what I had once seen—a thin dog with its back legs broken by a car, dragging itself around on its front legs until exhaustion or gangrene or thirst killed it. It might not be as bad as that, but I did not know. I did not even know where it was or how I could get to it. In the old days I should have taken a gun out and shot it. Now I had no gun and no authority to tell anyone to do anything. I could go out and find the dog and take it to someone who might do something. But I did not know who. I pictured myself going into the Civil Lines police station in the small hours with a broken dog wrapped in a hotel blanket, asking that somebody should shoot it. It was a fantasy I did not fully expect to realize. The crying went on. It was very near now. I got out of bed and made a move for my clothes. Then the crying turned to a squeal of terror, and the sounds went away from me. Someone, one of my daytime debaters probably, had had his sleep disturbed and had thrown something at the dog or gone for it with a stick. The crying went further and further away until it was out of earshot. I put my pajama jacket on and got back into bed. There was nothing I could do. There never had been much I could do, and now there was nothing. The fact that I no longer had any formal responsibility did not make it any better.

The room servant brought me a tray of thin tea and thick milk at seven with a copy of the new day's paper. The President, the Foreign Minister and the Governor had all made speeches, and a religious leader had urged a return to the spiritual ideals of Islam. They were all reported at length, but I had no heart to read them.

CHAPTER

5

I PASSED THE BEAUTY, STILL ALONE AT HER TABLE, AS I
came out of breakfast. She was not, by local standards, particularly young. I suppose in her early
thirties. She looked, like all the real beauties of that
part of the world, fragile and exquisitely neat. I
looked at her with a sort of deferential admiration.
I was too well trained to look at the women of the
country with anything but deference. She met my
eye very directly and then, as I came level with her,
smiled very slightly and said, "Good morning." The
voice was, as I had thought, throaty and the pronunciation, so far, exquisitely clear and correct. I
said, "Good morning" with, I suppose, pleasure and
surprise in my voice, but did not check my stride. I
was, in fact, both pleased and surprised. Not to
pursue the matter at that stage was instinctive.

Soon after I got back to my room the room bearer

came in and said, looking down his nose, that there was a gentleman to see me. The bearer was to some extent one of the old school, and I knew that look. It meant that the gentleman was hardly, judged by some standard of his own, worthy of my acquaintance, but he supposed I would see him. The ingrained reaction was always to express delighted readiness to see any gentleman, regardless of the bearer's views on his suitability, and this I did. A moment later Mr. Aziz was ushered in.

I knew at once why the bearer had disapproved of him. For one thing, he was, for the northern Punjab, very dark-skinned, and there is no one more color-conscious than the inhabitant of what we used to call northwest India. It has little or nothing to do with the comparatively short episode of European supremacy. It goes much further back—I suppose to the time when the conquering Aryans drove the dark-skinned Dravidians south, presumably keeping a few as serfs and prisoners of war. There is no caste in Islam, but there is an ineradicable association of a dark skin with social inferiority. In the villages in particular the hereditary menials were often several shades darker than the landholding tribes. There was something of sex attraction in it too. It was said that a young man's first requirement in his bride was that she should be fair-skinned—partly, no doubt, for social reasons but also because he fancied her better that way.

Also, Mr. Aziz was undeniably a bit flashy. There was nothing of the officer's subdued tweeds about him. His suit was a blue that only just cleared purple, his tie was gaudy. He had oiled, tightly curled black hair and his smile was brilliant. He came in with his right hand outstretched and his left grasping a splendid briefcase. I rather took to him. He said, "Good morning, Mr. Gilruth. It is very kind of you to have come all this way to help us. I hope you are enjoying your visit so far."

Not for Mr. Aziz, either, the Sandhurst voice. His English was fluent and persuasive, but wholly of the country.

I said, "Thank you. I'm still a bit confused, to tell the truth. It's twenty years since I was last here, you know. It's a long time."

"A long time, yes. And things have changed a lot, also. You will have seen that already, I think?"

There was no sense, with Mr. Aziz in front of me, in denying this. He was himself an unmistakable portent of that change. He was the new man in person, an almost clinical embodiment of a dramatically expanding commercial middle class. I did not know what his origins were, but I was ready to bet that as a boy he had run barefoot, and I wondered whether his shiny winkle-pickers hurt him as much as they ought to.

I said, "Indeed, yes. Of course, I've only seen Lahore so far."

"You have not been out of Lahore, Gujranwala side?"

"Not yet, no." Gujranwala is north of Lahore, the next district along the old Grand Trunk Road.

"I will take you and show you. There is great industrial development. Factories all along the road, both sides."

So, exactly, might a nineteenth-century mill-owner have spoken as the tide of smoke-blackened brick crept inexorably over the hills and fields of the midlands and the north. Only there was, to my way of thinking, not very much to spoil in the great flat, dust-colored stretch of country between Lahore and Gujranwala, and God knows the people needed the money. Also, in the late twentieth century, even in Pakistan, no industrial revolution could ever be as wicked or as dirty as the original explosion in nineteenth-century England.

"I should like to see it very much," I said. "It's very kind of you to suggest it. I haven't a car, of course, at the moment, but—"

"No, no. That's right. You will need a car. Later, at any rate. But I will take you in my car, if you would like that. You would like to go now?"

"Yes," I said, "by all means. I have no other plans. I expect we can discuss things as we go."

"Of course." He smiled at me expectantly and, when I got up, shot to his feet and stood there looking at me. I was wearing perfectly respectable tery-

lene trousers and an open-necked shirt. He said,
"You want to put on a coat?"

I did not want to, but was clearly expected to. I
said, "Yes, I think I'd better. Excuse me a moment."
I went through into the bedroom and put on a tie
and a thinnish jacket. Through the curtained doorway I could hear Mr. Aziz humming quietly to himself. It was an odd tuneless sound, but mainly it was
curious because humming to yourself was in my experience a Western trick. I could not tell at all what
he was supposed to be humming. When I emerged
through the curtains, he again looked me up and
down. He seemed to find me acceptable. He said,
"Good. We will go, then?"

"Lead on," I said, but he waved me out of the
door ahead of him. We walked together through the
compound. His car was a plum-colored Volkswagen, and he drove it himself. He shut me into the
nearside seat—Pakistan still drives on the left, and
the Volkswagen people were ready to oblige with
right-hand drives—and got into the driving seat
himself. He threw his briefcase, still unopened, into
the back seat, and we headed out into the noisy confusion of the traffic. Like most of his countrymen,
he was an uninhibited driver, and we took on all
comers on even terms. I did not think I could be
seriously injured at town speeds, but I was glad to
think I was so heavily insured. I thought about
Estelle. I had thought about her a good deal off and

on. I did not want her here with me, because whatever it was I had come to face, I could only face it
alone. But I wanted to be with her in London again.
Now I wondered whether she would really, as Toby
had said, rather see me back alive than have the in-
surance money. Ten thousand pounds is a high figure to put on yourself. How many women, as free
to please themselves as Estelle was—she had, after
all, no real stake in my future—could be offered the
choice between ten thousand pounds and their man
back and be trusted, in their secret mind, to choose
the man? For myself I did not think I minded very
much whether I lived or died, and I hoped Estelle
would be to some extent pleased either way.

Mr. Aziz turned down for some reason towards
the railway station. From there we skirted the edge
of the old city, crept under the tremendous bastions
of the fort and gathered speed past the white min-
arets of the Badshahi Mosque. I am not a devotee of
Islamic architecture. But Lahore, after all, had been
a Muslim city before the Sikhs took over the Punjab.
In the long perspective we had perhaps done no
more than turn out the Sikhs and restore the place
to its former owners. I certainly did not grudge it
to them, though I had always been fond of the Sikhs
as people.

As I remembered it, the Ravi Bridge had looked
raw, modern and unmistakably strategic, so that you
imagined long columns of marching infantry break-

ing step as they crossed it from one crenelated watch-tower to the other. Now it looked antiquated and, as the link between a capital city and its industrial suburbs, pretty clearly inadequate. The setting itself had not changed. The river bed was still a vast shallow trough scooped out of the plain. At this time of the year a single shining strip of the perennial river meandered through the middle of it, but later, when the rains fell and the snows melted on the remote invisible hills, the whole trough would be full of dark brown water, going like mad. It had to be a long bridge. Meanwhile, the lines of cars and buses and trucks crept impatiently across the ribbon of tarmac, and Mr. Aziz grunted and pushed his gaudy beetle towards the promised splendors of Gujranwala.

"You need a new bridge," I said.

I thought this would please him, but he seemed to take it as a disparagement. He bridled slightly. "It will come," he said. "The Jhelum Bridge, too. That is worse. There is too much traffic."

I was determined to make my point. I had no wish to try to put down Mr. Aziz. "It's the penalty of progress," I said. "We built this bridge. It was good enough in our day. It won't do now. You need something bigger."

This got through, and now he nodded, smiling. "So many things we need," he said. "But it will come." Then he frowned again. He said, "But first we have to pay for our war."

The factories were there, all right, one after the other, like the scheduled light-industrial area of a statutory New Town. They competed with each other in the impressiveness of their titles and the airy fantasy of their concrete façades. There was still, hearteningly to me, something left of the spirit which had made a tiny bazar workshop call itself the Imperial Cycle Works or the North of India Engineering Co. Only now the thing was serious. The capital, whether native or foreign, was there and the stuff was being made and, presumably, sold.

I said, "Where does the labor come from? The surrounding villages?" and this was just the cue Mr. Aziz wanted.

He turned and gave me a brilliant smile. He said, "That is it, that is it, do you see? These people have a regular income now. Before, as you will know, if the harvest was bad, there was no money. Or there was government service."

"Not so much here," I said.

"No, not so much here. But now one brother does the cultivation and the others go to work in industry. It is very much better."

"So long as someone does the cultivation. You still need the food."

"They do, they do. And prices are high, you see. And the yield per acre is higher too. But it is the industry that has made the real difference. In other parts, where there is not much industry yet, it is more as it was."

I said, "Fazilpur, for instance?"

He flashed me a quick questioning look, neither smiling nor frowning. Then he said, "Fazilpur, yes, certainly." It was the first time the place had been mentioned between us, and it was I who had mentioned it.

He swung the car suddenly off the road and into the gate of a long low factory. It was in pale blue washed concrete with the name Jehangir Products in red along the ornamental cornice. He said, "We will just go in here." We pulled up under a fretwork *porte-cochere*, and a porter in a khaki uniform came down the steps and looked at us with a sort of puzzled melancholy. Mr. Aziz said, "Is Mr. Ahmad in?" and the man said, "Yes" as if he was confessing to something he was a bit ashamed of. Mr. Aziz said, "Good." We left the car standing in the shade, and he marched off down a long verandah. I went after him. There were work noises through the tall opaque windows on our right, and the air-conditioning fans were already humming gently. We came to a door marked Office, and Mr. Aziz stood aside and ushered me through it ahead of him.

A saturnine young man at a desk looked at me guardedly, but when he saw Mr. Aziz behind me, he smiled and heaved himself to his feet. They greeted

each other and Mr. Aziz again inquired for Mr.
Ahmad. The young man said, "Yes, please go in."
They spoke formal Urdu, and all the time the young
man looked at me intermittently out of the corner
of his eye, but Mr. Aziz did not introduce me or explain my presence. I remembered the feeling so well.
Nothing and no one was ever explained unnecessar-
ily in this country. Etiquette did not demand the
meaningless introductions of the West, where nothing could be done until everybody had heard and
forgotten everybody else's name.

I had no idea what Mr. Aziz was at, but it did not
seem to matter. It was his time. I went along with
him, wondering when I was going to be called on to
do anything. I was reminded, again, of my first arrival in the country. I had been sent out on tour with
a very bustling revenue officer, who just got on with
his job, with me trailing anxiously behind him.
Every so often he would break off and explain to me
in English what was going on, but he never, so far
as I could understand, explained me to anyone else.
Then I had been sunk in a feeling of guilt and inad-
equacy, because I was supposed to be responsible
for all this and my pay was already three times his.
All I could do was to look keen and watchful and
try to pick an occasional whiff of meaning out of
the torrent of Punjabi. Now I had a sense of positive
irresponsibility, and could at least understand most
of what was going on. So I trailed behind Mr. Aziz,

looking pleasant, feeling mildly amused, and waiting.

Mr. Ahmad was a plump, balding man. He did not seem to be expecting Mr. Aziz, or to be surprised to see him. I had a feeling that Mr. Aziz was a more than usually active dropper-in in a country where dropping in was very much a part of life. We all sat down, Mr. Ahmad behind his desk and the other two of us in front of it, and they exchanged the usual courtesies in Urdu. Mr. Ahmad suggested tea, and Mr. Aziz turned to me and said in Urdu, "You will drink tea?"

I said, "Yes, thank you very much"—it was a thing you never refused—and Mr. Ahmad turned and said to me in English, "So you speak Urdu?"

"I used to. I have forgotten, but I hope I can get by."

I had stayed in Urdu, and Mr. Aziz said, "Mr. Gilruth was out here in government service before Partition." Mr. Ahmah rolled an eye at me, nodded and said nothing. They plunged into a business discussion. The stilted Urdu went gradually by the board and the language took on the smooth flexibilities of Punjabi. Tea was brought, and the small formalities over the tray brought me and Urdu back into the conversation.

But Mr. Ahmad was plainly not what I had been brought out to see. He knew nothing about me, nor I, at the end of it all, anything about him except that he managed this factory, where they made different sorts of small mechanical components, and that he had occasional dealings with Mr. Aziz.

After a bit Mr. Aziz said, "Well, we must be going," and we all got up. We all shook hands politely and Mr. Aziz ushered me out. The saturnine young man nodded from his desk but said nothing.

Outside we turned in a different direction, and presently Mr. Aziz opened a door and led me into one of the shops. It was a typical light-engineering shop. I had seen lots like it in England but none here. There was the same background noise of machinery and the same atmosphere of leisurely but fairly purposive activity. There was nothing of the black satanic mill about it. I thought again, as I had thought earlier, how lucky a country was to postpone its industrial revolution until well into the twentieth century, even at the cost of a few more slightly underfed generations. To have preserved the subcontinent as a market for our manufactures was not a thing we were ever likely to get, or indeed deserve, much credit for. It might nevertheless be one of the more substantial fringe benefits of our rule. Mr. Aziz pointed expansively to the labor force. He was like a commissar pointing out to the foreign visitors the merry peasants singing at their work on a carefully stage-managed collective farm. I nodded my appreciation. We did not attempt speech in competition with the machinery.

Back in the plum-colored beetle, he suddenly spoke to me in Urdu. "Well," he said, "you've seen it. There's a lot of difference, isn't there, as I said?"

"There is indeed. And your idea is that what has been done here must be done in Fazilpur too?"

"That's right. You'll see when you get there." He had switched suddenly into the western Punjabi they speak in Fazilpur. Alone of the dialects it makes its future in the good Greek style by adding S to the root. It was nice to hear it. "All right," I said. "I'll see when I get there. God knows whether I shall be able to speak their speech, though."

He turned and gave me one of his careful, noncommittal looks before his mind went back to his driving. He said in English, "You used to speak it very well." He dropped me at the hotel and drove off with a friendly wave. We had made no further appointment to meet.

noisier and more lugubrious. I ate a *kofta* curry with
yellowish greasy rice. The hotel's Pakistani food
was like the poor ghost of Oriental cookery that
used to be put up by English cooks before gastro-
nomic enlightenment hit England. Its Western food
had clearly been cooked by an ambitious but undis-
cerning Oriental. It seemed to me that they ought
to be able to manage one or the other, but they fell
heavily and regularly between two stools. I ate what
I needed because I had to, but got little pleasure out
of it. I ordered green tea instead of coffee because
I thought it might come in handy as a digestive. It
was thin stuff, even so. The band was playing "I
Can't Give You Anything But Love, Baby." I tried
to remember whether it had first come out before
or after my time out there, but no time scale seemed

to apply. When the vocalist came in, his thin, handsome Punjabi face produced, not very successfully but still disconcertingly, the sort of noises native to an American Negro. I wondered what had led him to this occupation and what he really thought about it. The performance was applauded mainly by his fellow countrymen. The foreigners heard it out in slightly patronizing embarrassment. I got up to go, picked my way through the tables towards the door and met the solitary beauty coming to the door from the other side of the room. I had not seen her dining. She gave me a very cheerful smile and said, "Good evening."

The band soared into a crescendo, and I shouted back at her, "Good evening!" When we both got outside I said, "It's a bit noisy, isn't it?" For all I knew, she might like it, and I didn't want to say the wrong thing.

"It's terrible," she said. "I don't know why they want to make so much noise." Her English was unaffectedly perfect, even to the flat unrounded O's. Her voice was a marvel. It was as if she was going to burst into birdsong as soon as she finished speaking. I wanted very badly to hear her laugh and wondered what sort of thing she might be inclined to laugh at.

I said, "I should think to take people's mind off their food." I wondered, even as I said it, if it was safe, but already I could not see her as a person you had to be careful with.

She turned and smiled up at me. She was not very tall, but her hair was piled up on her head and the clothes gave her height. She said, "That's pretty terrible, too, I'm afraid."

"Afraid?" I said.

"Well—I felt some apology was required. You're a visitor, aren't you? I'm a Punjabi. I think we ought to be able to do better than this."

We walked out into the cool of the compound. The wide leathery leaves hung motionless in the yellow lamplight, and the drivers squatted and smoked by the waiting taxis. There was not a breath of air stirring. She set off towards the opposite end of the compound, away from my room. I walked with her, though I was not sure whether this was in order, and prepared myself for a smooth and polite disengagement when we got to the door. But she said, "Come in and talk for a bit, unless you've got anything else you ought to be doing."

A servant who had been sitting in the verandah got up and held open the wire mosquito doors against the spring as we went in. He seemed to take me very much as a matter of course. The sitting room was the same as mine, but it had been cleaned by her servant, and there were flowers and things of hers about. It smelled very slightly exotic, whereas mine smelled only of dust and varnish.

I sat in the chair she pointed to and she sat oppo-

P. M. HUBBARD

site me, across the low round table that was part of
the local furnishing tradition. I said, "I'm not really
an ordinary visitor. At least, I've been out here before. I was a government servant out here in the
old days."

"Really?" she said. "Were you in the I.C.S.?"

There was something very English about this.
The initials, once a combination to conjure with,
were very much forgotten now, even in a country
that still went in a lot for English initials. Nothing,
of course, with the word Indian in it could be allowed any long currency. I said I was, and she
mentioned the names of several people I remembered. They must all have been a lot older than she
was. She said, "My father knew them all. I remember the names. And what some of them looked like.
I was a child, of course."

"Was your father—?"

"My father was in politics," she said, and I asked
nothing further. After a moment she said, "My
husband's an engineer. He's Irish."

It is difficult to explain at all, and quite impossible
to explain logically, how important this was to me.
The best that I can hope for is that it will at least
make it clear that the way I felt about the women
of the country had nothing to do with color bar
and was, indeed, not properly a racial thing at all. It
was, as I have said, some part of an official ethos
which we had inherited from the more elaborate

rectitude of an earlier official generation. You were conditioned, I suppose, to look at the Punjabi women in a certain way, perhaps rather the way in which a Catholic priest is taught to look at all women. You saw, constantly, their beauty of face and figure and at times their physical desirability: but you were not on their wave length. Their attraction was not for you. For you it was the English colonel's wife or the English commissioner's daughter, even though, compared with the women of the Punjab, the one was blowsy and the other raw, and both in their way badly spoiled by the too facile command of male attention.

If this very English-minded beauty had been, as I had assumed, the Begam Farid Khan or some such, the mental barrier, even now in these wholly different circumstances, would have taken a great deal of breaking down. As soon as I knew she was Mrs. Lambert, she became simply the beautiful wife of an absent husband, staying in the same hotel as I was, with the compound full of breathless trees between her door and mine. Morally I do not suppose there was anything in it. But that was the way it worked.

All I said was, "You don't live in Lahore, obviously?" I do not know whether she felt the mental change in me. She probably did. It is a change very few women miss, this sudden focusing of conscious desire. If she connected it with her admission of an

Irish husband, she probably attributed it to the assumption, common to the country, that Christian wives were much more accessible than Muslim wives. Her manner did not change at all.

"No, no," she said. "But my family home isn't far from here. That's why I come here sometimes when Patrick's away. But we live in Pindi. He has one or two projects up there. Only at the moment he's in Europe. He'll be back in a week or so. I'm going up to Pindi in a day or two to get the place straight."

"I'm going up there myself pretty soon."

She gave me a very long look, always with that same small smile playing about her mouth. I still had not heard her laugh. She was wonderfully sweet and very dignified. The elaborate hair style contributed to both. "Are you?" she said. "When?"

"I don't know, in fact. I'm out here on a job of sorts, and I suppose I'll go when I'm sent." I was quite clear in my mind that the oddities of Mr. Carruthers of London and Mr. Aziz of Lahore were not for discussion with any third party, even one as sympathetic as this. She for her part did not ask about it. She did not, after all, know that I was now by trade a writer. To her I was an ex-administrator, and a job of sorts that brought me out here was natural enough.

She said, "I'll give you our address and telephone number. Then you can come and see us when you get there. Would you like that?"

She said us, not me, but I should still like it, and I said so. She wrote the address and number on a tear-off pad and passed it over to me. She had a firm, round, rather schoolgirl hand, like many of her English contemporaries. She said, "You don't play bridge, do you?"

"Not really, no. No, I don't."

Quite unexpectedly she laughed. It was an enchanting sound, throaty and full of tremendous good humor. I looked at her, smiling from the infection of her laughter, but waiting to be told the joke.

"I think I know what you mean," she said. "You mean you can, but you won't unless you're fairly sure what's involved. You're quite right. I won't either. I was taught bridge—it was part of our education. But I'm not getting myself involved in bridge at Pindi. Especially the women's bridge. Patrick's always on the look-out for players. When he asks you, you'll have to make a more convincing job of it. Or shall I tell him firmly in advance that you don't play? I'll say I've asked—I don't know your name—"

"Gilruth."

"I've asked Mr. Gilruth to come and see us. He used to be I.C.S., but he doesn't play bridge. Is that right?" She ended the question with a little interrogative sound, which I suppose should be written "eh?" but which was in fact very un-English and altogether charming. I have said that her English was perfect. By this I mean the words she used and her pronunciation of them. Her voice and the way she used it, a good deal of her inflection, were of her own country. I found the combination entirely irresistible.

"You do that," I said. "Then perhaps we can talk while the others are playing bridge."

We smiled at each other. "Not in the same room," she said. "Patrick wouldn't have that."

"In another room, then."

"All right. I'll make it a sixsome, with two non-bridge-players. Then we can talk—in another room."

"Mostly," I said, "you talk and I'll listen. You do it so beautifully."

She said, "Oh—" on a descending note. She still smiled. She was not in the least arch or coy, or even on-coming in the way a European woman might have been. She was just full of a sort of bubbling delight, which she seemed eager to share. Only of course I had no idea how far this participation in delight might extend.

We talked a little longer. She found out a certain amount about me, though never, so far as I can remember, by direct questioning. She never asked me my business in Pakistan. At one point I asked her— I forget what led to it, but the question seemed natural enough—if she had a family. She said, "No children, no. Patrick and I agreed. I don't think it's a good thing, even now, with a mixed marriage. Though a lot of people do it. I think it's different if the father is Pakistani. All sorts of people now have foreign wives. It's quite the thing." She smiled to herself, as if there was something that amused her but might not amuse me. I looked at her, challenging her to include me in her smile, but she would not be drawn.

Finally I said, "Is that fairly recent? It was very rare in my day. Apart from the landlady's daughters who married Indian students they thought were princes. And that didn't generally last long, not once they got out here."

"I think it must be. They're an interesting lot, I must say, the foreign wives. Patrick is very funny about them sometimes. Not all English, of course. In fact, mostly not. Americans, Swedes, Germans. But all fair, you see—all blondes. I think that's still the attraction. But they manage things so differently. And manage their husbands differently, too. Patrick says you can tell what nationality his wife is before you've been ten minutes with a Pakistani married to a foreigner!"

When I got up to go, the servant, who had been sitting in the verandah, opened the wire door to let me out. I do not know how much English he understood—I suppose in that household quite a lot—but it was all innocent enough to listen to. Whether it was not in fact wholly innocent I simply did not know. My suddenly established relation with Mrs. Lambert was something completely new to me. It had been established on her initiative, not mine; and I had so much pleasure in her company that I would have settled for its indefinite continuance on the same terms. She was a person, I thought, with whom your mental relation would remain very much the same, whatever happened physically—and that not from any shortcoming in the physical transaction, but because the mental relation from the start was extraordinarily vivid and sweet. She was like something in a dream, but one of the achingly innocent dreams of adolescence.

She held out a small cool hand and said, "Well, Mr. Gilruth, we shall meet again in Pindi anyhow, I hope. You'll let me know when you get there?"

I held the hand, Browning-wise, only a little longer than a friend might and said I would. As I backed out into the dark verandah, the strand of sudden extraordinary affection stretched between us and went with me tenuously, like a gossamer, so that I was never wholly separated from her until I went to sleep. I did not see her at breakfast, and after breakfast Mr. Aziz came to visit me in my room.

He came in, as he had before, with his smile carrying all before it and his hand outstretched. "So," he said, "you would like to go up to Pindi now, I think?"

I connected this immediately in my mind with Mrs. Lambert, but realized at once that there was no connection in his. "I'm at your disposal," I said. "You tell me what you want me to do, and I'll do it as best I can."

He seemed to brush aside the suggestion that he should instruct me. He said, "You know Pind Fazl Shah very well, I think?"

"I used to. But I expect that's changed too."

He shrugged. "Not so much as here. It is more old-fashioned. The roads are better than they were, of course. You will not need a horse, I think." He gave a little giggle. "You used to ride everywhere in the old days." He seemed to think about this. "The officers do not ride now," he said.

"We used to have to put in a monthly return of miles ridden," I said. "But they didn't pay us any sort of horse allowance, as far as I remember."

"They do now. Of course, it is more expensive, keeping a horse. And the officers make the returns, I expect. But I do not think they ride." He said this in a perfectly matter-of-fact way. He was very much the private businessman talking about civil servants as I suppose businessmen talk about civil servants all over the world.

"Anyway," I said, "I haven't been on a horse for twenty years, and, to be honest, I shouldn't very much like to try."

He smiled cheerfully. "There will be no need, you see. The area we are interested in is not so large.

There will be a car for you, and where a car cannot go it will be easy to walk."

"Can you tell me what the area is?"

"I can tell you, certainly. It is an area stretching southwards from Pind Fazl Shah. There are villages called Bhagrian and Daud Faizu and Kallar Kot. There are others too." He was looking at me with great intentness and for once he was not smiling. He said, "You remember them, perhaps?"

There were small bells ringing in my head, but I could not bring what I wanted to the front of my mind. I shook my head. The faintest suggestion of a smile returned to his mouth, but his eyes remained very watchful. "I think I remember the names," I said, "but I can't say I associate them with anything special. What are you aiming to do, and where do I come in?"

He paused for just the fraction of a second. I got the impression that he was wondering just how far he ought to take me at this stage. Something, some degree of disingenuousness, was obvious, but I did not know what it was all about. Then he said, "We —that is to say, the people I work for—wish to acquire land along a particular line for some works they have in mind. We cannot acquire the land except by buying it. There is no compulsion. It is in the interest of the people themselves that we should develop this project. You know that—we have already discussed it. But they will not perhaps all understand that."

I thought I had begun to see something of what lay ahead. My mental comparison with nineteenth-century England had not been so far out. The canal companies and later the railway companies haggling and brow-beating their way across country at a time when private enterprise could buy what it wanted only in an excited market. I said, "What are the works to be, then?"

He said, "You see, I am not an expert in these things. But I think there is to be a road and a pipe-line. But our people there will tell you all that."

"You won't be going up yourself? You know that part of the country, don't you?"

We looked at each other for the first time with almost undisguised caution. "Oh yes," he said, "but my job is mainly here at Lahore. But you will go—will the day after tomorrow be convenient?"

I gave it up. "Whatever you say," I said, and he was all smiles again.

"That is good," he said. "I will tell them."

7

I WENT UP TO RAWALPINDI, IN THE END, BY ROAD. IT
was a run I had done often enough in the old days,
and I wanted to do it again, even if I was not going
to be allowed to drive myself. I asked Mr. Aziz to
cancel my air ticket and get me a seat on a seven-
seater minibus belonging to the government trans-
port service. I did not see Mrs. Lambert again before
I left, and do not know when and how she got back
to Rawalpindi. I imagine she had her own car and
driver, but she did not suggest giving me a lift.
That would have made a very different journey. I
parted from the hotel without regret. I tipped my
room servants what I hoped were the right amounts
—I had no need to be economical on my employers'
money—and was given to understand by their reaction that what I had given was tolerable but not
spectacular. I had still not got over my old ideas of

what a rupee was worth, and had continually to refer it back arithmetically to an equally depreciated pound.

The taxi driver was an older man with a saturnine lip and a starched military turban. I took him for one of the village youths I had seen being taught to drive army trucks in Hitler's war. He picked his way through the riotous traffic with cautious and rather sour disapproval. He was the kind of man you met occasionally in England who had somehow failed to climb on the bandwagon of national infla-tion because instinctively he disapproved of it, and then made his disapproval explicit because he had failed. He took my Urdu for granted. Unlike the younger men, he had been used to talking the stiff army Urdu to Englishmen in the old days. He shook his head gloomily and said, "A lot of cars."

"A lot of money," I said, and he looked at me over his shoulder with increased interest.

"A lot, sir," he said. "Everybody's got it." Except me, he meant, except me. "I tell you, sir, a man whose father hadn't got a bullock cart now has three cars in the family."

"It's the same with us," I said, "only we didn't even have bullock carts."

He nodded. "You were in the army?" he said.

"No, I was a civil officer."

He sucked his teeth as though it took all sorts to make a world. Did I know a Colonel Miller of the

79

Punjab Regiment? I said I was afraid not, and he nodded as if his worst fears were confirmed. But he told me about an amusing correspondence he had had with Colonel Miller in the years after the war. He had hoped the Colonel might come out and see him, but he never had. I listened, showing my appreciation at the proper intervals. This sort of friendship had been the backbone of the old Indian Army, a simple backbone of essentially simple men. I had never ceased to think that the Indian Army was the best thing we ever did in India. When we got to the bus station, I told him to put me and my suitcase down at the gate. It made it easier for him to get his car away, and I felt it would sadden him to see me, even if I was a civilian, carrying my own suitcase and finding my seat in a minibus. I tipped him with tactful lavishness for the sake of the old days and Colonel Miller. He saluted, sardonically as ever, and took his cab back into the bedlam of present-day Lahore.

With one exception, my fellow passengers were all men of what I took to be the new middle class. They looked the same as the clerks and shopkeepers in the old days, but they were very different mentally. I do not think this was only my imagination. They were busy, confident, not particularly talkative, polite to each other and me. I expect most of them had some English, but I spoke to them without hesitation in Urdu. There was a social line, which I was beginning to recognize, between the people I could talk Urdu to and the people who would take it amiss if I did not talk to them in English. This had little or nothing to do with linguistic ability. It was just that above the line it was the thing to talk English, whereas below it it was a matter of convenience. If I got it wrong and went into Urdu with the wrong person, I was firmly taken back into English, even though my Urdu was at least no worse than his English. The exception was a distinguished-looking elderly man who had the front seat beside the driver. I did not know what he was. He was already in his seat and took no part in the small exchanges as we all got settled.

We crawled out of Lahore in the afternoon heat, picked up speed beyond the Ravi Bridge and settled down to work off the last hundred miles of the plain, first between the factories and then through the vast mottled levels of cultivation. To the moving eye, nothing had changed here at all. This was the Grand Trunk Road of Kim and the marching redcoat regiments, clean through from Delhi to the frontier, with every blooming camping ground exactly like the last and nothing but trees and the small, occasional works of man to break the huge monotony of the plain. I was anxious to get through with it, but now suddenly apprehensive of what lay ahead. Lahore, which I had never been much concerned with, was already all the world away.

Rightly or wrongly, I had given part of myself to Fazilpur, and that was where I was going. As the sun went down I gathered my irresponsibility around me like a blanket, but already I felt the cold.

The bus stopped at Gujrat, and we all got out to stretch our legs and drink a cup of tea. When we were waiting for the bus to start again, the front-seat passenger drifted up to me and looked at me with a sort of shy authority. He had a magnificent head. The skin was almost hairless and corn-colored, drawn tight over lean, beautiful features. He said, "You must excuse me, but I heard you speaking Urdu, and I was interested. You are English, I think?" His speech went with the rest of him. With its rounded vowels and delicate inflections, it might have been the voice of an elderly Celtic don.

I agreed I was English, and he said, "Ah, then you will have been a government servant out here before Partition." He looked at me with careful detachment. "Yes," he said, "you are just old enough, I think. It is twenty years ago. But I don't think you can have been out here very long before Partition came."

"Not very long, no."

"I thought not. And now you have come out to write a book about us."

"Not primarily. I might, I admit. I do write books."

"Yes, yes. What were you out here? A judge,

would it be?"

"I was a magistrate and revenue officer mainly."

He nodded. "Have you been in any of the courts since you returned?"

"Not yet. I am hoping to."

"You will find them very little changed, outwardly. The same courts, the same law, the same procedures. It is remarkable, really."

"Yes?" I said. "Yes, I was told it was all very much the same."

He held out his hand suddenly and shook mine gently. Then he turned and started getting back into his seat in the bus with the deliberate, calculated movements of old age. He said half over his shoulder, "The justice is not the same."

I climbed into the bus after him. There was no one else there yet. I stood, stooping slightly under the low roof, behind the seat where he sat gazing out throught the windscreen at the turmoil of the station yard. I said, "It was far from perfect in our day," but he shook his head at this.

"It is not the same," he said.

The driver swung into his seat and put his finger on the horn button. I heard one of my fellow passengers with his foot on the step behind me. I wanted to say something more to the old man, but this did not seem the time or the place for it. And he had shaken hands to say good-bye to me. I sat down in my place and waited unhappily for the bus to get on the road again. The justice is not the same, I thought. God knows, it was never an easy country to be just in, but I suppose most of us did our best in a groping sort of way. The old man ought to have comforted me, but the further we got north, the more my depression deepened.

There is a point somewhere between Gujrat and Jhelum where the road suddenly goes slightly uphill. If you have done most of your driving in a part of the world like western Europe, it is difficult to understand the strangeness of this. Something solid shows in the dust haze on the horizon ahead, and the road suddenly heaves under you. All this time it has lain like a railway track before and behind, and now suddenly it rears up and climbs a small natural ridge. Then there are little ragged hills on both sides of the road, not more than twenty feet high, scrubby, use-less to anything but goats. The fact remains that you have finished with the plain. This, ultimately, is going to be the Himalayas.

It was dark long before we got to Rawalpindi. We twisted and climbed through line after line of the bare hills. We saw their jagged edges against the last of the daylight and then against the brilliant early stars. Finally, sunk in the chilly lethargy of the long, uneasy drive, we saw the lights spread-eagled on the ridges ahead of us. We never touched the old city, but hooted our way in through the squared-up streets of the cantonment bazar. I tried to have a word with the old man in the front seat, but I missed him in the confusion. I still do not know who or what he was. He cannot ever have guessed how bitterly, before the thing was over, his parting shot remained with me.

This was a sharp upland air, utterly different from the oppression that blanketed the plains. I intervened in a hand-to-hand struggle between two trap drivers for my suitcase, and surprised myself more than them by shouting them down in their own language. They were the lean, rangy type I remembered, full of natural gaiety and potential violence. I paid off the winner with a certain amount of badinage at the hotel. My depression had gone for the moment. I felt, more keenly than at any time since I had left Karachi, that I was nearly home. There was a good deal of apprehension in it still, but a strong, almost physical exhilaration. The hotel was no better and no worse than Lahore, and this time I was prepared for it.

I got in to a late dinner, and the first person I saw when I came out was the Major. He was in the bar with another man, similarly dressed but much younger. Even from where I was I could catch the masterful cadences of Sandhurst. The other was much quieter and more hesitant. I could not hear his voice at all, but from the way he used his mouth you could see he was talking a different sort of English. I was tired and hoped I should not catch the Major's eye, but before I was even abreast of them, he had fixed me. He tilted his face back with an expectant smile on it and raised a powerful brown hand. It might have been a kind of salute, but it looked as if he was going to reach out and grab me if the smile did not stop me.

I turned aside, unwillingly but smiling into his smile, and went up to them. The Major said, "Hullo, my friend. Had enough of Lahore, eh? I'm afraid I never got your name. Silly of me."

"Gilruth," I said.

The Major held out the hand he had waved at me with. "Nazir Ahmad," he said, and we shook hands solemnly. The boy—he seemed little more than a boy to me—bowed formally and said, "Akbar Khan."

"I met Mr. Gilruth on the plane from Karachi," the Major said to him. "He's here on business, but he's been out here before."

Akbar Khan said, "Have you been here long? This time, I mean." His English was very clear and wholly without frills. The face was young and sensitive, but the mouth firm. He was the nicest kind of young man. There was no real harm in the Major, but the boy showed him up like an X-ray.

"No," I said, "only a few days. You're army, too, I take it?"

The boy said, "Yes," and the Major said, "Akbar's just joined us. But he comes from these parts, any-

86

way. He's a wild Awan."

"Are you?" I said. "Where is your home in fact?"

"It is a village called Kallar Kot, in the Fazilpur district."

It did not take me more than a moment or two to trace the connection. I said, "Ah, in the Pind Fazl Shah direction." The boy was simply pleased, but I saw the Major look at me a little sharply. I thought that, like most people with an elaborate act, he probably had a mind very different from the one you were supposed to assume. I had no intention of discussing my Fazilpur business with him, at least not until I knew a lot more about it—and, perhaps, about him. I said to the boy, "As Nazir Ahmad's told you, I've been out here before. But tell me how things are in the villages. I've only really seen Lahore so far—cars and factories, you know what it is. Are things as prosperous in the villages?"

I thought he hesitated slightly. Then he said, "Oh, not too bad, I think. We haven't got any factories so far, but I don't really think we're very keen to have them. The farmers do very well at present prices. And there's a lot of army service, too."

"You think you're better off as you are?"

He wrinkled his guideless brow in a desperate effort to be honest, but he smiled all the time a small deprecating smile. He said, "*We*'re all right. We're landholders. It's the other people who'd benefit most, of course. The tenants and so on. But it would turn everything upside down. I don't know. My father won't hear of it. But then he's one of the old school."

"Is there any particular project under discussion?"

"Oh well—there's been some talk of developments at Pind Fazl Shah that would affect us. But my father won't hear of it. They won't get him to agree to anything, I know that."

"He was an army man too, was he?"

"Oh yes. Served his whole time. We're all—we've all been army, more or less." He was suddenly very solemn. He said to the Major, "I think I must be off. Thank you, sir." He gave me a formal bow and went off, very slim and erect, between the little tables and out into the foyer.

The Major looked after him. We both did. I said, "What a nice boy," and the Major nodded.

He said, "He lost his elder brother—well, half-brother, really. Grand chap. He became a martyr in the war."

It was the first time the Major's English had deviated from its chosen norm, and I knew he did it deliberately. I felt sure he knew half a dozen jolly army phrases for being killed in action, but he was not going to use any of them. All Pakistanis killed fighting the Indians were *shaheeds*, martyrs of Islam. The thing did not translate easily into Sandhurst English, but he was not going to let it go.

I said, "I'm sorry. I didn't know, of course. The

father's still alive, though?"

The Major was back in form. "My goodness, yes. Wonderful old boy. Subedar Major and Honorary Lieutenant. All the decorations under the sun. A.D.C. to the Viceroy. You know the type. Well in his eighties now, but straight as a ramrod. And a real old diehard, of course."

"Akbar's young to be a son of his," I said, and the Major almost winked at me.

"Well," he said, "you know how it was. The old man married a young wife—what?—well in his sixties, I suppose. Akbar's her son. We can't do it now, you know. The President's stopped that one. Can't take a second wife now without the consent of the first. Not much chance of getting that, though, is there, eh? What do you think?"

He laughed his clubman's laugh and I joined the joke as best I could. "I hadn't heard that," I said.

"Oh yes. Well—it's right, of course. Made all sorts of trouble."

"That I know. I've seen some of it."

The Major nodded. "I dare say," he said, but his mind was already on something else.

I said, "Well, if you'll excuse me. I'm pretty tired, in fact."

"Of course, of course. We'll meet again, I hope. Be here long?"

"I don't know yet. A week or two, I expect."

"Good. Well, we'll meet, then."

We waved to each other and I walked back to my room. There were no trees in the compound here, and the air moved briskly between the blocks of buildings. Kallar Kot, I thought, Kallar Kot. It was not one of the names I remembered from my time at Pind Fazl Shah, but there was something there that nagged at the back of my mind. But I was too tired to think clearly tonight. I slept twice as well as I had in Lahore.

A YOUNGISH MAN CAME TO SEE ME NEXT MORNING. HE was tall, dark and extraordinarily impersonal. He said, "Good morning. Mr. Gilruth? I am Mr. Fabri's personal assistant." He did not say who Mr. Fabri was. I was expected to assume, as I did, that he was Mr. Aziz's local boss. Unless they had done something very funny with his name, he could hardly be a Pakistani.

I said, "Good morning. Am I to have the pleasure of seeing Mr. Fabri?"

"Yes, sir. That is what I have come about. Mr. Fabri would like you to call on him tomorrow morning. At about ten, Mr. Fabri says."

"Certainly. And by the way—Mr. Aziz seemed to think there might be a car I could use. It would be a convenience, I must say."

"Yes, sir. I have it here, if you would like to see."

I wanted to see very much. It was a Morris-1000 tourer, not new, but quite spruce. Pakistan went in for cars of several different nationalities, but the middle run seemed to be all Morris-1000's or Volkswagen beetles. It would do me very well, and I said so. The young man said, "You can drive it?" I said I could. I had an English license and an international one. Would that be all right? He said, "Surely." He pointed to where she stood in the hotel compound. "You may leave her there," he said. He collected what was obviously the driver of the Morris, and they put themselves into a Mercedes and disappeared with polite salutes. I got into my new possession, put the seat right, fiddled with the controls and started the engine. It sounded all right. I put the keys in my pocket and went back to my room. Then I picked up the phone and asked them to get me Mrs. Lambert's number.

I think I hoped to hear that throaty voice of hers at the other end of the line, but I got a servant. It seemed wrong to ask for the memsahib, but I did not see what else I could say. The servant took it calmly enough, but said the memsahib was not in. She would be in at lunchtime. I decided to leave a message. I did not think I should be here at lunchtime. I asked him to tell her that Mr. Gilruth, whom she had met in Lahore, had arrived in Rawalpindi. I left it at that. Then I went and asked for something in the way of a packed meal. They said sandwiches and a bottle of beer in ten minutes' time. In fifteen minutes' time I was heading out on the Grand Trunk Road for Peshawar. The hood was down. The air was fresh and full of pale yellow sunlight. I was alone with the strange broken country that had been so much part of my mental background before I had buried it all in the moist grey-green of England. I was going to Pind Fazl Shah, but I did not believe I should ever really get there. Pind Fazl Shah was something in my past mind, not a place a measurable distance along a tarmac road; and you can never go back to your past mind, even if you want to, which most of us do not.

At least they had not taken down the Nicholson memorial. I remembered it as you saw it at sunset, standing up very dramatic against the yellow sky in the gap where the road went through the wall of hills. In this mild sunlight it looked rather old-fashioned and incongruous, like all the other stone memorials of the illustrious dead who seemed to have been overtaken a little by history. But then I did not expect anything to be as I remembered it. I did not think I could face it if it was. I myself, or at any rate the self that had left Pind Fazl Shah twenty years ago, was one of the dead, though not an illustrious one. I did not want to see the memorials of my dead self exposed in this bright unwavering sunlight. I did not think I wanted to be remembered at all. At least I did not want to meet anyone who re-

membered me. I was here on a purely private ren-
dezvous with my old innocence, and I did not
reckon to have any third party present.

Much later I turned off the main road, making
direct for Pind Fazl Shah and avoiding Fazilpur.
Fazilpur had been, and still was, the district headquarters. To me it remained the headquarters of
Mackinson, who had been deputy commissioner
when I was sub-divisional officer. Mackinson was
one of the successful ones. If the end had not come
when it did, he would in time have become en-
trenched in Lahore. As it was, he had since done
well for himself in industry. He was patient, able,
immensely charming and immensely canny. He had
encouraged me, restrained me and refused to take
me or my enthusiasms very seriously. He had in
fact been a very good D.C. to work under, if only
I had been capable of learning the sort of lessons he
had to teach.

When I first saw the name Pind Fazl Shah on a
milestone, I did not fully believe it. The milestones,
which looked like medium-sized whitewashed
tombstones, had the names in the Arabic script. I
wondered whether they had in the old days, but
found I could not remember. On the whole, I
thought not. It seemed odd that they should have
bothered to Arabicize the milestones, which a foreigner might want to read, when every other notice
in the country was in English. Further back along

94

the road, somewhere near Jhelum, I had seen from
the minibus a dusty side road, full of camel trains
and the familiar droves of broken-hocked donkeys
staggering under their enormous loads as the boys
beat them forward. The road had been marked FOR
NON-VEHICULAR TRAFFIC ONLY. I had wondered
what the camel drivers and donkey boys were supposed to make of it. But Pind Fazl Shah was marked
up in Arabic, though the figures were Roman.
There was only fifty miles to go. I still did not
believe it.

I did not remember this road at all. I suppose I
had driven over it in the old days, but not very
often. Coming this way, you did not get into the
sub-division until you were only a few miles from
Pind Fazl Shah. I had left it very seldom during my
two years, and never for very long. It was, I suppose, about half the size of Northern Ireland, and
whatever happened in it, I had been responsible. I
was very young at the time, and when you are
young, these things weigh on you. When I had left
it, I had generally made for Fazilpur, and the Fazilpur road did not join the one I was now on until
near the boundary.

I knew what I ought to have done. I ought to
have written a polite little note to the present
S.D.O., said who I was and asked if I might call on
him. Then, although I did not expect a reception
committee, there would probably have been one or

two people who remembered me, and we could all have had a cheerful talk about old times. But I did not want this. I supposed I should have to pay a ceremonial call on my remote successor, but not until I had had my own private meeting with the place first.

When I did come to it, it was all appallingly sudden. One minute I was in unknown country, though of a familiar type. The next I was suddenly running down a narrow road which I had not thought of for God knows how many years, but which was as familiar as the back of my hand. The road dipped down between the lines of acacias, and I knew that beyond the bend it ran out on to the river crossing with Pind Fazl Shah on the far side. The river bed was dry most of the year, a beaten-up wilderness of boulders and sand with low cliffs on each side. When enough rain had fallen in the right places, the water came roaring down it, but unless there was a great deal of it, it went through the culverts where the road ran on a built-up causeway. The road was seldom cut for long, and a bridge was out of the question. I had once, on urgent business, had to swim a similar river between Pind Fazl Shah and the southern half of the sub-division, but such drama was not usually necessary. Now I drove slowly, and with an appalling reluctance, through the empty, shut-in wilderness, and set the Morris at the slope between the cliffs on the far side.

There, straight away, it all was. I did not think it could have changed much. There was the bunch of official buildings, all in color-washed brick. The S.D.O.'s bungalow, the courthouse, the revenue office, the police station. There were others further back, and beyond them the flat, piled-up roofs of the town itself. I pulled the car on to the soft yellow dust at the side of the tarmac and switched off. The silence was almost complete, but there was a faint murmur of men's voices. In one or more of the buildings along the road the business of government was still proceeding. In front of them, under every tree, even along the sides of the road, there were people waiting. They waited in groups, muffled in their sun-bleached clothes, squatting with their staves over their shoulders, sitting, lying on their backs with one knee drawn up. Waiting for something they had been told to wait for, orders, decisions, relief, even justice, something at any rate they could get nowhere else and could only wait for. There had always been people waiting, and there they still were. For a panic-stricken moment I believed that they had been waiting for me for twenty years, while I was away, occupied with other things and forgetting the rights and wrongs of it. I had only to get out and walk towards them, and they would be around me at once, demanding my attention, thrusting out their professionally written petitions with the long mauve rupee stamp at the top. Someone would say, "He's come," and the word would spread from group to group, and the liers would sit up and the sitters struggle to their feet, and people would run and call to each other, because there might not now be so long to wait for whatever it was they were waiting for. But in fact I was only a ghost, come back, like all ghosts, to haunt only myself, and even if they saw me, I would mean nothing to them. There was nothing I could do for them now, and I did not know whether to laugh or to cry about it.

In fact, of course, I did neither. There was really nothing to laugh at, and the sort of person I now was very seldom cried. But I got out and walked slowly up the road towards the buildings. The bungalow had had a purdah compound of mud brick built out on one side of it where there used to be the remains of a mud tennis court. I did not go there, because all the indications were that the S.D.O. was in court. I walked over towards the courthouse. No one took much notice of me. I was an object, I suppose, of mild curiosity, but I had no apparent significance. There was nothing in me for anybody, and they let me go by without comment. I moved the split-cane curtain aside and put my head into the courtroom. There was a criminal case in progress. The whole picture was immediately recognizable because it was substantially unchanged. The police wore different uniforms, and on the wall behind the magistrate's chair the hatchet face of Mr. Jinnah, looking curiously like an Edwardian Englishman in his stiff white collar and narrow tie, had replaced the mild benevolence of His Late Majesty the King Emperor. Otherwise I could see no change at all. I had walked into the back of many courtrooms while a case was being tried, and here I was again. The voices went on softly, heads were bent over notes and files, the thing was by Western standards curiously intimate and informal. I sat down on a chair against the wall. I had been here before, and could wait as well as the next man.

Presently someone noticed me, and there was a murmured word, and an orderly came back down the long room and asked in a polite whisper what I wanted. I wrote on a slip of paper, "I should be very grateful for a few minutes' interview, but there is no urgency at all. Please do not let me interrupt proceedings." I signed it with my name but nothing else. I did not think for a moment anyone would recognize it. There were two or three pleaders in court, but none of them was nearly old enough to have been practicing in my day. The orderly took the paper back and handed it to the magistrate. The magistrate gave me a nod, and one or two heads turned in my direction. Then they went on with the job.

Presently they could get no further. I knew all the symptoms. The pleaders and the police prosecutor shuffled their papers together, the police guard gathered up the accused, the magistrate gave them a date for the continuation of the case and pushed back his chair. The orderly came halfway down the room and beckoned to me. I got up, exchanged a polite good-afternoon with one of the pleaders and joined the S.D.O. in his retiring room. He was a little man, a little puddingy, with small darting intelligent eyes. He was older than I had been when I sat here, but not all that much. He greeted me in cautious English and asked me to sit down.

"I've really only come to pay my respects," I said. "I was S.D.O. here myself before Partition, and of course I wanted to see the place again."

He said, "Indeed?" His eyes went to my name on the slip of paper but could make nothing of it. "That is very interesting. You are just visiting Pakistan, or you have some work here?"

I knew that if I told anyone, it ought to be the S.D.O. He would find out soon enough in any case, or would if he was doing his job properly. I have very little doubt that the reason I did not was that I knew so little about it myself. That had been my reason for caution all along. The suspicion was growing in my mind that there was something here I had not been told about because I might not like it. Until I knew what it was, I was not going to admit to anyone, not even the man (at least by my standards) most concerned, that I was mixed up in the thing at all. I said, "Well—I am a writer by profession. I certainly hope to write something as the result of my visit. But of course I wanted to see Pind Fazl Shah again in any case." It was true as far as it went, and I was being no more disingenuous with him than other people had been with me.

He said, "I see, I see." He looked down at the slip of paper again. "I feel I should know your name, but I'm afraid I cannot recall it."

"Why should you?" I said. "Certainly when I was here I couldn't have told you the name of an S.D.O. twenty years before me. It will be on some of the old files, I expect. But one doesn't often go as far back as that."

"No, that is true." He seemed grateful for my fellow feeling for him in his job. "You have come from where today?"

"From Pindi. And I must be getting back there. But I shall come out this way again, I hope."

"Yes, you must do that, certainly. And please let me know. There must be people here who remember you, I think."

"I will, of course. I ought to have let you know before I came today, but I came rather on the spur of the moment."

"That is right. Then if you come again, I can make suitable arrangements."

I got up and he got up and held out his plump hand. He was a soft little man altogether. Much softer, I thought, than Mr. Aziz, who did not hold charge of a country half the size of Northern Ireland and full of lean wild men who killed each other on very little provocation. "Good-bye, then, for the present," he said.

I do not know what made me say it just then. There were plenty of other people I could have asked. But as I shook his hand I said, "Oh, by the way, which way is Kallar Kot from here? I used to know, but I can't place the road."

He dropped my hand and stood there looking at me. There was nothing sudden or dramatic in this. It was just that I had made him think. If I had no particular business in the sub-division, why was I interested in a particular place? He said, "You want to go there?"

"Some time," I said. "I know it's not far from here, but I find I can't remember where the road takes off. I'd like to go down that way a bit." I tried to make it sound like a sentimental journey. I did not know how far I had convinced him.

He said, "I see. Well—the road runs south from the town. If you go from here to the town, there is a turning off to the left before you get into the bazar."

"Yes," I said, "yes, I think I remember it now. I'll find the road, at least. Good-bye for the present, then, and thank you." He bowed me out. It occurred to me afterwards that I did not know his name, but this would be public property.

I walked back through the courtroom, and a waiting orderly saluted me as I went out of the door. I returned the salute solemnly and walked back to my car. I found the road easily enough, because I remembered it before I got there. The day had clouded over suddenly. This country was made for sunlight, and without it its essential gauntness was a little forbidding. I never thought of Pind Fazl Shah except in bright sunlight. The road wound on between the irregular patchwork of fields, tailored to the contours of a broken landscape. The villages and hamlets stood on their mounds, partly natural, partly the accumulated debris of generations of mud-brick houses. I had been driving for some time when the road dived into a ravine. The thorn trees grew along the top of the water-worn cliffs on each side. It was very narrow, and in that sickly light there was something very menacing about it. The ravine ran down into another seasonal river bed. The village on the far side was Kallar Kot. I knew it at once, but could not understand why the whole picture was so familiar. There it all was, the village on its mound, the river bed sprawling below it, and to the right, downstream from the road, a track slanting down from the center of the village. The track, in particular, was clear in my mind. I stopped the car where the road ran out of its ravine on to the empty river bed, and as I got out I remembered what it was. It was the Kallar Kot murder case. Three figures hurrying down that track in the dusk and a fourth, possibly a fifth, running after them. This was where it had happened.

I backed the car gingerly on the narrow road and set course for Pind Fazl Shah and Rawalpindi.

CHAPTER

SUBEDAR-MAJOR FAZL DAD KHAN CAME TO PAY HIS
first formal call on me a couple of days after I had
taken over the sub-division. The formal call was an
established part of district administration. It was a
harassing one, on occasion, for the officer called on,
but it had its value. The regular time for it was the
early part of the morning, before the courts and
offices open at ten. To be a caller on the local officer
was to claim a certain social or official status, though
this was never defined. If you were not up to calling,
you got a petition drafted and put it in the box outside the courtroom. Then you were presently sum-
moned to speak about it in the courtroom, with
clerks and other people present. But a caller had a
private interview at the officer's house. He did not
by any means always have anything special to say.
Half the time all he wanted was to meet the officer

(particularly, of course, a new man) and impress
on him who he was and what he had done and what
he wanted next. The thing was to some extent an
exercise in status, though in those days the word
was not as much rubbed as it is now. Every caller,
like every other man in the sub-division, had his
private axe or axes in his pocket and might, if the
occasion seemed right and the officer sympathetic,
take one out and grind it a little. But only a minority
of callers came with the set purpose of grinding a
particular axe. You got to know the look of these
and often, when you were under pressure and time
was running out, spent a lot of ingenuity and patience trying to get them to admit that they had
something in mind and tell you what it was. This
was specially trying when you already knew what
it was, but could not bring them to admit it existed.

Subedar-Major Fazl Dad Khan was a caller pure
and simple. His rank and service entitled him to a
personal meeting almost on demand. He was also, in
fact, a pleasure to meet. He did not wear uniform,
but on this first occasion he wore his tremendous
array of medals on his formal coat. They were real
medals, won in real fighting anywhere from Af-
ghanistan to Flanders. The sad, oversimplified thinking of a later day could, I suppose, call him a co-
operator or something of the sort. The truth is, he
was a professional soldier, content to serve with
dignity under a race and government that had dem-

onstrated its military superiority. And of course he was a romantic figure, as Housman's soldiers are romantic. He embodied all the old splendor of soldiering, which is built on loyalty, but has far less to do with patriotism than a nationalistic age tends to assume. We made friends then, and I saw him at regular intervals thereafter. He lived his own life and was not an obtrusive public figure, but he was always there. A man like that was immensely valuable in that system of very personal administration.

He was in his sixties then. I never saw a finer physical type in finer condition for his age. I remember hearing, the way you did hear things, that he had taken a new young wife. If it was undignified, it was the only undignified thing I ever knew him to do. Anyhow, the law allowed it and nobody could doubt his ability to do his duty by her. He no doubt kept his senior wife in order, and the girl might have been a lot worse off. You assumed he had sons, and you assumed they were, or would be, in the army. I had not in fact ever seen a son of his when the blow fell.

I received the first report of a murder case from Bhagrian police station. The clerk who put it up to me looked very solemn, and I asked him why. Murder was common in that part of the world. Good administration consisted not in preventing murder, but in catching and punishing the culprit and so preventing the incident from becoming the first link in a chain reaction of lawlessness. A riot or armed robbery was much more serious than mere murder, even if no one got killed in the course of it, because it was a public flaw in the fabric of law and order. Murder was a private incident. The clerk said the case had been registered against Bahadur Khan, the eldest son of Subedar-Major Fazl Dad Khan. The Subedar-Major was a man entitled to respect, and this was serious. The fact that the murdered man was one of the village menials made it either more or less serious according to your point of view. The circumstances were all too familiar.

Bahadur Khan had seduced the daughter of an oldish man who was the hereditary blacksmith of Kallar Kot. When I say he had seduced her, I mean that he had persuaded her to run away with him. Seduction or abduction was the national sport of the young bloods of the landholding tribes. It was not by any means confined to the women of the menials. It was a criminal offense under the Indian Penal Code. Once they had got the woman away, it was in fact almost impossible to obtain a conviction; but it had to be taken seriously, because to local sentiment the thing was a flaming affront to the honor of the woman's family and, given any chance at all, the affront was going to be avenged sooner or later. There was a local proverb which said that men got killed over money, women or land. The three Persian words all began with a Z, and it made a nice jingle. There was not much money in the Pind Fazl Shah villages, and the land disputes were pretty rigorously channeled through the revenue courts. But the women claimed their victims regularly. In this case the killing was on the wrong side to start with, which made it worse.

The blacksmith had arrived at the police station late at night, leaving his elder son dead on his bed at home from a spear thrust that had partially disemboweled him. The stationhouse officer was an energetic character and honest, as these things went. He had taken the story straight and registered the case immediately. The picture that came through was a recognizable one. The blacksmith was sitting outside his house smoking in the dusk. The menials' houses were all together on the edge of the village. His daughter had gone out, as the women did at dusk, to relieve her bodily needs in the fields around the village. This was primordial custom. The land around the village, thus enriched, was specially productive, and was subject to a higher rate of land revenue. Somebody had come running and said, "Your daughter's gone." The blacksmith had been confused, but his elder son, a boy of seventeen, had caught up a stave and gone running in defense of the family honor. He had run down that long track towards the river bed, and his younger brother had run after him. At the bottom of the track he had come up with the runaways. There was a girl in a

burqa and two men with her. One of the men had
hurried on with the girl, but the other had turned
to meet the pursuer with a spear. The blacksmith
found his elder son dying on the track. His younger
son was by him, crying. He was only ten or there-
abouts. The girl had gone.

If the stationhouse officer had been a less honest
man, he might have done one of two things. He
might have reported no identification at all, or he
might have reported several eyewitnesses, including
the blacksmith, all ready to swear to the culprit's
identity. As it was, he reported what was almost
certainly the truth. No one had seen the thing but
the small boy. The small boy was said to have recognized the killer as Bahadur Khan. There would no
doubt be supporting evidence, but purely on the
matter of the abduction. There would be people to
say they had seen Bahadur talking to the girl. He
was missing from the village. But there had been
two men with the girl, and only one of them had
done the killing.

All this was for me a matter of advance information only. It was for the police to get their case together and decide how to proceed. The case would
come to me, as Sub-Divisional Magistrate, when it
was ready. I could not try capital cases, but I had to
conduct committal proceedings. This meant that I
should hear the complete prosecution evidence and
then either discharge the accused for lack of proof

or commit him to stand his trial before the Sessions Judge at Fazilpur. The Sessions Judge was a Hindu member of the I.C.S. several years senior to me. He was a nice chap to talk to, but as a judge I found him a bit unpredictable.

My heart went out to the Subedar-Major, but of course I did not see him. He knew I could not meet him when the case was pending, and, as in honor bound, he kept away from me. But I heard that he had himself gone after his son, wherever he had got to, and brought him back and produced him before the police. The police arrested him, and the next day I had an application for bail presented in my court by an advocate practicing at Fazilpur. The Subedar-Major still did not appear, but through the advocate offered to stand surety for his son's appearance in any sum I liked to fix. I asked the police prosecutor what he felt, and he turned up his eyes and smiled a little ruefully. Bail was not usual in murder cases, but the Subedar-Major had produced his son once and it might please me to suppose that he would, if bound, produce him a second time. I allowed bail in five thousand rupees, which was quite a lot of money then by local standards. Bahadur Khan was released to his father's surveillance.

I did not remember all this at once. It came to me piecemeal during the days that followed. What I did remember, now that the spring was released, was the committal proceedings and what followed them.

111

Even then the Subedar-Major never appeared. I
heard he was at Kallar Kot, shut in his tall brick
house and refusing to see anyone. Bahadur Khan
appeared with his counsel. I could not remember
what he looked like, but I know that even then my
impression was not wholly favorable. He was too
typically the son of a notable father, with the father's inherited qualities somehow offset by the relationship between them. I remembered the blacksmith as well as I remembered the Subedar-Major.
He was a small stocky man with a dark pug face.
He looked, and probably was, of a different race
from the tall, olive-skinned Awans, and he had none
of the Subedar-Major's nicety of conduct. He way-
laid me outside the court and put his turban at my
feet, begging for justice on his son's murderer. I
replied with the standard formula. I said, "Father, a
decision will be made according to the evidence,"
and then my orderlies hustled him away. The evidence, the only evidence that counted, was the evidence of the boy. He was a very intelligent boy,
but with a child witness that cuts both ways. The
more intelligent, the more easily schooled. They put
a stool in the witness box for him to stand on. He
stood there, very bright-eyed and solemn, and
through the bars in the front of the box I could see
his toes wiggling. We all had a go at him, the police
prosecutor, counsel for the defense and myself.
Everyone was conscious of the High Court's rulings

about child witnesses, and everyone handled him gently. There was no question that as soon as the girl was known to have gone, Bahadur Khan was generally held responsible. He had evidently been indiscreet in his preliminaries. I did not think there was much doubt that the boy had run after his brother when his brother had caught up his useless stick and run to get his sister back. The question was whether the boy had really been near enough, in the dusk, to see the killer clearly, and, if so, whether he had recognized him as Bahadur Khan or merely had the name put in his head afterwards. He was questioned, of course, about his previous knowledge of the accused. He said simply he knew him by sight. He lived in the village and he had seen him around. Everything he said was simple. The boy was not simple at all. There was precious little to cross-examine him on, and cross-examination made very little impression. At the request of the defense, the court adjourned to the scene of the killing. We stood there on the track, with the wind ruffling our papers, while they argued whether the boy could in fact have seen what he said he had seen. When we returned to Pind Fazl Shah, the prosecution closed its case. Defense counsel offered no evidence and asked for a discharge. This was on a Friday. I fixed the case for orders on Monday. I waited in my retiring room, doing routine stuff, until I was certain everyone would have gone home. Then I walked

across to my bungalow with the file under my arm
and the decision like a ton weight on the back of my
neck. I had two days to think about it, but there
was precious little thinking to do. Whatever it ought
to have been, the decision was very far from being a
purely judicial one. I was desperately concerned
with the rights and wrongs of it. They were full of
contradictions.

Here was a poor man, with an inherited social
inferiority, who said he had had his daughter stolen
and his son killed by the raffish son of the local big-
wig. I was, by traditional title, the cherisher of the
poor, the local fount of justice and equity. The
blacksmith wanted justice. The fact that the evidence was weak meant nothing to him. He was certain Bahadur Khan had killed his son, and he looked
to me to give him redress. Seeing things, and myself,
as I saw them then, I found this desperately difficult
to refuse. On the other hand, there was the law. The
law itself had a claim, and it was a claim that
weighed a lot more heavily with me than it did
with some of my colleagues. If I shut my mind to
what everybody assumed but could not prove, as
the law required me to do, I had to admit that the
evidence against Bahadur Khan was very doubtful.
I was half inclined to think that the boy was speaking the truth, but I had seen child witnesses before,
and I was rightly afraid of them. Lastly, there was
the Subedar-Major. For the son I cared little but the

Subedar-Major was a man who commanded my respect and affection. Moreover, he had a claim on me
and whatever it was I represented. He was a faithful
servant of the government whose work I was there
to do, and he had been specifically fighting my
battles when I was an infant, and even before I was
born. He was a much more reasonable and experienced man than the blacksmith, but he would
believe passionately that he had this claim on me;
and to send up his son on a murder charge on very
slender evidence would be to fling his claim in his
face.

This was a personal problem much more than a
problem of applied justice. It was doubtful, even if
I committed Bahadur Khan, whether the Sessions
Judge would convict him and the High Court up-
hold the conviction. I did not know what the Sessions Judge might do—I had, as I have said, found
him unpredictable—but I knew the High Court. In
a similar case with different people involved I might
have taken the easy path of committing on the assumption that at some point there would be an ac-
quittal. But there was no easy path in this case.
What I was concerned with was the administration
of the sub-division—my sub-division. It was my
decision that mattered there, and it seemed to me
that whatever I decided would do it harm. I longed,
of all improper and irrational things, to talk to the
Subedar-Major and explain my predicament to him,

115

but there had been no chance of this. I was desperately concerned and very unhappy. Of course I was alone with my concern and my unhappiness, but that was nothing new.

I put the thing out of my mind on the Friday evening by reading a mixture of Shakespeare and Dorothy Sayers. On the Saturday evening I went out for a long desultory walk. When I had got back and bathed and dined, I went through the file again. I made nothing of it, because it was not there my problem lay. I went to bed early and tired, and slept. I was wakened by someone coming very quietly into my bedroom in the dark. I did not know what time it was. There was very little to prevent this. I was entitled to a police sentry, but had long ago dispensed with him. There was not much worth stealing, and no one had any reason I knew of for wishing me physical ill. Anything was better than to have the sentry tramping around the house when I was trying to sleep, coughing at intervals to show me that he too was awake. I never systematically bolted my doors. Anyone could walk in if they liked, only up to then no one seemed to have wanted to.

A voice whispered, "Sahib," and when I put on a torch I saw the Subedar-Major kneeling on the rug at the side of my bed. His turban was on the floor beside him. He was quite bald. His face was clean-shaven except for the fierce grizzled mustaches. He looked older than I had ever seen him look. I put the torch out and whispered to him to get up and put his turban on. I got up and put on a dressing gown. I took him through into the sitting room and made him sit down. I did not put on any lights. It was a clear night outside, and we could see each other well enough. I said, "Well, Subedar-Major Sahib?" We never got above a whisper.

He said, "Sir, my life is in your hands. Let my son go."

"Did he kill the boy?" I said.

He hesitated, but replied with what seemed perfect candor. "I don't think he did. I think it was the other man, the one who was with him. He killed the boy. My son did not wish it."

I said, "You know you should not have come. If anyone knows you came here—"

"No one will know, unless you tell them."

I gave it up. "What then?" I said.

He said again, "Let my son go. You can do it. The evidence is not much. I am an old man, but the rest of my life is at your service. Only let my son go. I have served the government all my life. In return I have some medals and a pension. I have never asked for anything else. Now I do ask."

I got up and he got up and stood in front of me at attention. He was a fine man and old enough to be my father. I held out my hand and he caught it between both of his. I said, "I haven't made up my

117

mind. Go now, please, and go quietly. I must think before I decide."

He said, "Think carefully, Sahib. My life is in your hands." Then he saluted and went. I did not hear a sound once he was outside. The next day, Sunday, I got the car out and drove into Fazilpur to see Mackinson.

I got there about noon. He was sitting back in a long chair on the grass in front of his house. There were bottles and glasses on a table. He smiled at me as I came to him across the grass, but he did not move. He said, "Hullo, Gilruth. Get yourself a drink and sit down. What about this Kallar Kot business?"

I said, "I'm afraid that's what I came to see you about."

"You've heard the case, haven't you? Have you committed?"

"I've heard it, yes. I've reserved orders for tomorrow."

"And you don't know what to say?" He seemed, as he so often seemed when we discussed district matters, mildly amused. I envied him the decisiveness that went with this detachment, but the detachment sometimes jarred on me as if it was irresponsibility. I can see, now, that he was not in fact irresponsible, only he did not get emotionally involved as I did. I suppose it was really a whiff of his emotional detachment that I had come all that way to pick up if I could.

I said, "No, I can't make up my mind."

He looked at me very straight, but spoke gently. "It's for you to decide," he said. Then he smiled again. "Ten to one old Gupta will acquit anyhow," he said.

"I know, but it's my decision that matters to me."

Have you spoken to old Fazl Dad?"

I could not answer this truthfully. What had happened last night was between the Subedar-Major and myself. I said, "He hasn't appeared at all."

"He wouldn't. He's a decent old so-and-so." He sipped at his glass, held it up to the light and sipped again. "Look here," he said. "All I can say is this. It's your case. But people like old Fazl Dad have a claim on us. It would knock him for six to have his son tried for murder, especially in Gupta's court. And I wouldn't put it past Gupta to convict in a case like this. If the evidence is there, you must commit, of course. But if there is any real doubt, I wouldn't want Fazl Dad hurt." He quoted the Urdu proverb which says, "A friend to my friend, an enemy to mine enemy." "Anyhow," he said, "do the best you can and don't worry yourself sick over it. There's too much going on all the time for that."

The next morning I discharged Bahadur Khan. The Subedar-Major was at the back of the court. He said nothing, but before he went out with his son he stood up very straight and gave me a crashing military salute. The old blacksmith said, "Your Honor, what sort of justice is this?" The court

119

officials hushed him and bundled him out before I had the need or the opportunity to say anything. I wanted to explain my predicament to him, too. But you cannot explain everything to everybody—even, half the time, to yourself. The small boy was there. He stood for a moment or two after his father had been conducted away, looking at me with bright sardonic eyes set in a poker face. I still did not know what to make of him.

I had never seen the blacksmith again. The Subedar-Major had come to see me once before I left the sub-division, which was fairly soon after the case. He had not stayed long or referred to the case directly. He had pressed my hand and repeated what he had said to me in the small hours when we sat facing each other in the darkness. "I am an old man, but the rest of my life is at your service." I had not thought of him from that day to this. He had been buried with all the rest of the innocence and uncertainty. But now, driving back to Rawalpindi twenty years later, I remembered him, and wondered.

CHAPTER

10

I HAD NOT BEEN LONG BACK IN MY ROOM WHEN THE phone went. It was the voice that earlier I had wanted so badly to hear, Mrs. Lambert's voice. But now I was still not fully back in the world she seemed to belong to; and there was something in the tone of the voice, even from the start, that worried me. She said, "Mr. Gilruth? It's Mrs. Lambert here. I had your message."

Then she simply stopped, and I did not know quite what I was expected to say. Finally I said, "Yes, well, you said I might get in touch with you. I only got in yesterday evening."

"Yes. My husband wants me to ask you to dinner."

Something was obviously badly wrong, but I still did not know what. I said, "That's very nice of him, but—"

"No, but you see, he doesn't know I've met you. I hadn't mentioned it. I was going to, but then he suddenly said you were at the hotel and he wanted me to ask you to dinner." She stopped speaking for a moment. When she spoke again, her voice was as brittle as a flawed glass. She said, "I didn't know you knew him. You never said so."

"But I don't," I said. "Do please believe that. I suppose—I suppose he must be something to do with this business that's brought me out. But I didn't know he was. You do believe that, don't you?"

She said nothing for a moment. Then she said, "If you say so. I want to believe you. I don't know what your business is. You didn't say."

"I didn't say because I'm beginning to think I don't really know myself. What did your husband say?"

"Nothing much. He never says anything much about his work. But I—I don't know, I didn't very much like the way he spoke of you."

"But he doesn't know me," I said. "At least, I don't see how he can. Look, can't we meet and talk about this?"

"Yes, I think so. Yes, all right." She paused. "Look," she said, "do you know the bookshop at the corner of Rawlings Road in Sadr Bazar?"

"No, but I can find it."

"Well, it's a big shop, and one can be looking at

books. I'll be there tomorrow morning at eleven."

I thought. "All right," I said, "I've got to go and see a Mr. Fabri at ten. I should be clear of him before eleven."

"Mr. Fabri? Do you know Mr. Fabri?"

"Not yet. Do you?"

"Oh yes. He works with Patrick."

"He does, does he? Well, look, I'll go and see him as arranged. And then if we can meet later, perhaps I'll be able to tell you more about what's going on."

"All right. Mr. Gilruth, I'm sorry. I thought—"

"I know. It was at least partly my fault. But I'm pretty well in the dark myself. You do believe that?"

"Of course." The voice was full of warmth now.

"Bless you," I said. "Tomorrow at eleven, then."

She said again, "All right," and rang off. I sat down and let my mind go back to Kallar Kot.

I was trying to remember my conversation with the Major in the hotel bar the evening before. I was certain he had not mentioned the name, but the man he described as Akbar Khan's father could surely only be the Subedar-Major—my Subedar-Major. If he was, Akbar must be the son of his late marriage. The half-brother, who had been a casualty of the September war, could then, I supposed, be the same Bahadur Khan I had discharged twenty years ago. If so, he had made a good end. But he must have been getting on for a middle-aged man. I did not know how old he had been at the time of the case, but I remembered him as a young man in his early twenties. And I did not think he had been in the army then, or he might have had something better to do than running after the village girls.

In any case, from what Akbar had said, his father was a determined opponent of whatever the developments were that I was supposed to be reporting on. This might be coincidence. After all, if I had not happened to go to Kallar Kot that day, I should still not have remembered the Subedar-Major's existence. The fact remained that if my inquiries were to cover Kallar Kot, I was bound to meet him sooner or later, and presumably equally bound to be made aware of his views in the matter. I had gone to Kallar Kot, not because of anything Akbar Khan or the Major had said, but because Mr. Aziz had told me that it was one of the villages to be covered by my survey. It was pure chance that I had heard of the Subedar-Major's views before I went there. I wondered more than ever what would emerge from my meeting with Mr. Fabri. I also wondered whether to tell him at any point what I now knew of the Subedar-Major's views and what I had now remembered of my previous relations with him. I decided that I would have a good look at Mr. Fabri and hear what he had to say first. Unless the S.D.O. had passed the news back—and it would certainly be significant if he had—I did not see how anyone in

124

Rawalpindi could know that I had already found my way to Kallar Kot, let alone that I had rediscovered my particular relation with Subedar-Major Fazl Dad Khan.

I spent a desperately uneasy evening. The cloud which had come down before I got to Kallar Kot had never lifted. It looked as if we were in for a spell of spring rain. The great virtue of this was that it postponed the onset of the real heat, but that was not of much interest to me. This was a country for brilliant light, or at worst moving cloud shadow. Under a grey sky its essential bareness and savagery were evident and oppressive. My mind ran on what I had remembered, and I was wretched with useless and contradictory regrets. I found it quite impossible to recognize the person who had left Pind Fazl Shah twenty years before as myself. I knew that it was my fault that he had been the person he had been, and still more that he had become the person I now was. But if I was still subject to the obligations, and entitled to the rights, of my dead self, it was only in the way an heir takes over credits he did not himself earn and debts he did not incur—because he recognizes the inescapable processes of inheritance, not because he accepts them as immediately valid for and against him as a person.

I spent some time in the bar, hoping that the Major might appear, with or without Akbar Khan, but he never came. I drank three small shots of very doubtful Scotch at an utterly fantastic cost to my employers. This, and being invited to dinner by Mrs. Lambert, seemed to be the nearest I could get to living it up, James Bond fashion. At least there was no debating society outside my bedroom window here, and I slept deeply. I woke to a keen air, and when I went out, I saw that there was fresh snow on the pine-covered hills that fringed the northern and eastern sky. The heat would not reach Rawalpindi yet awhile.

At ten I went to see Mr. Fabri. His office was two floors up in a new concrete block where the cantonment ran out into the Sadr Bazar. There were no frills about Mr. Fabri. At least he did not make a mystery of the thing, which I was glad of. I was beginning to get a little tired of mysteries. He was neither Pakistani nor English. He was a foreign businessman, square, pale, and darkhaired. He wore gold-rimmed glasses. There were men like him everywhere now. There was nothing particularly sinister about him. I fancied that I, as an old imperialist, was more of a curiosity to him than he was to me. He regarded me, not without a certain mild amusement, as a pretty doubtful investment. This at least gave us something in common.

He got through the preliminaries quickly and then said, "Mr. Gilruth, it is considered possible that you may be in a position to help us. That is, if you are willing to do so. I myself do not doubt your

willingness, because I think you still have the interests of these people at heart, and what we are doing
will be very much to their advantage. As to your
ability to help us, that is a thing of which I am
anxious to be persuaded. We have brought you out
here on the advice of those who are already persuaded of it."

I thought this was more like it. I said, "I was told
in London that I was wanted to sound out local
opinion on whatever it is you have in mind."

He smiled. "That is, I suppose, in a sense true. In
fact, we are already fairly well acquainted with
local opinion. But—"

"You want some of it changed?"

He looked at me very seriously now. He said,
"Some of it must be changed. We have no power to
compel agreement. We can pay for what we want,
and in most cases that will serve. But not in every
case." He thought about this for a moment, staring
down at the front of his desk as if I wasn't there. I
thought he was probably an unusually single-
minded man. Then he roused himself and came back
to me in the bustling breezy style of the senior officer briefing his subordinates on an operation which
he wants them to believe in as well as understand.
He unrolled a map across the desk, stubbed down
at it here and there with his finger and reeled off
figures at me. It was, as it was meant to be, an impressive performance. Only it was mostly wasted,

because I was ready to be persuaded of the virtue of the proposals once I knew clearly what part I was expected to play and found it acceptable. If my part was what I had now begun to suspect, it did not seem to matter very much whether I shared Mr. Fabri's vision or not. I did not even listen very carefully, because my mind was suspended on what was to me the logically prior point. But there was to be a big manufacturing plant on a site for which they already held options just outside Pind Fazl Shah. From there they were to drive a road and a pipeline in a more or less straight line through the villages to the south as far as Khanke Pattan, where there was a railway junction and also a perennial water supply from the river. It was cement primarily and what Mr. Fabri called "other products." I found myself looking at the map while Mr. Fabri's words flowed over me. Their broad strip between its black dotted lines ran clean through the eastern half of the Kallar Kot lands. All over the strip, right across the map, there were little patches hatched in in red. In most of the villages the red hatching more or less covered the strip. There were gaps here and there, and a conspicuous gap, almost the full width of the strip, in Kallar Kot. I wondered whether they had really, as I believed, brought me out from London to help them get the red hatching across that vital, obstinate gap. It seemed a curiously unrealistic thing to do, and I was not surprised at Mr. Fabri's barely concealed skepticism. But I saw him shrugging his shoulders and deciding that anything was possible in this unreasonable country. He was a man who would play a chance if he did not see a certainty. If I was right about this at all, I knew two things. I knew that somebody had suggested to Mr. Fabri that I should be sent for; and I knew that whoever it was had some fairly solid reason for making the suggestion. It was not all that unrealistic.

My eyes were still on the map, and I realized that Mr. Fabri had stopped talking. I looked up at him and he, still standing, looked down at me earnestly through his gold-rimmed spectacles. I pointed to the gap in Kallar Kot. I said, "That's where local opinion needs changing most, by the look of it."

He frowned at this, as if I was not playing fair with him. He said, "But I have not explained—"

I pushed my chair back and got up. "You haven't explained what the red hatching stands for, no. But we can skip that, surely. Should I be wrong in assuming that this area here—" I put my finger on the Kallar Kot gap again— "represents the holdings of Subedar-Major Fazl Dad Khan? I was out at Kallar Kot yesterday. I remember a good deal about the village now, but I'm afraid I can't be expected to remember where the Subedar-Major keeps his lands."

He nodded in a resigned sort of way. He said, "So you were there yesterday? Did you speak with

129

Fazl Dad Khan?" Of all odd things, the thing that
struck me was how well he pronounced the name. I
did not suppose he had been in the country very
long, but here he was with a painstaking imitation
of the local pronunciation instead of the take-it-or-
leave-it approximation of the Anglo-Saxon.

"No," I said, "I haven't seen the Subedar-Major
yet."

"Then—" he said, but I shook my head at him. I
did not see why I see should not be allowed to have a
mystery if I wanted one. It was my turn. There was
also, I suppose, a rather childish wish to show him
that the ex-imperialist still knew a thing or two and
was not going to be pushed around more than he
wanted. I saw no need to tell him that I had met a
man by chance on a plane at Karachi and again by
chance in a hotel bar in Rawalpindi. I had been on
the spot before he expected, and I already knew
what he had been intending to break to me gradually after a suitable build-up. "One hears things," I
said.

He looked at me blankly, while his no doubt very
agile mind made a reappraisal of the situation. Then
he smiled. I should not have been surprised if he
now, on reconsideration, saw more possibilities in a
thing which he had agreed to without much conviction. But he was not going to admit any change
of course. He said, "Well, Mr. Gilruth—do you
think you may be able to help us with Fazl Dad

Khan? He is not a very reasonable man, I am afraid. He is opposed to change on principle."

"He must be a very old man," I said. "Well in his eighties, I should think. A certain amount of unreason is to be expected, surely. What makes you think I should be able to make him see reason?"

"That is what I have been told," he said. "You will perhaps be able to tell. If you will at least speak to him—"

"I think I should want to do that anyhow. As for trying to persuade him—you do understand, don't you, that I must make up my mind about that?"

"But, Mr. Gilruth, this thing must come. It is very much in the local interest."

"And presumably in yours?"

He swept this aside impatiently. "Of course," he said, "of course."

"It's a bit odd, isn't it? I've still got to find out what the people want. But not to inform you. To satisfy myself."

"Satisfy yourself by all means." He was suddenly very chilly. "But, Mr. Gilruth," he said, "you have your return ticket. We are not keeping you here."

"No," I said, "all right. But I don't think I can simply let it go. Not yet, anyhow."

I was very angry when I got outside. I was back with the old emotional involvement, and it did not make sense. Pind Fazl Shah was no responsibility of mine; and there was no Mackinson now at Fazilpur to look at me with gently amused detachment over his Sunday-morning gin.

I found the bookshop easily enough. It was an extraordinary shop. Nearly all the books were English. There was a quite modern but wildly mixed stock spread over the tables and lower shelves. Above it, shelf on shelf to the high ceiling, there were hundreds of books which looked as if they had been imported and stocked before Partition and hardly moved since. I wondered who was supposed ever to read them now. Thrillers and romantic novels of the twenties and thirties, serious books about things which had long since lost any significance. The confusion had its attractions and gave you ample excuse for browsing. I blew the dust off a hard-back Edgar Wallace and was reading it with reminiscent admiration when I saw her come in at the opposite door. She drifted in my direction and said, "Hullo, Mr. Gilruth! Any of your books on sale?"

"I haven't seen any," I said. The assistant who had been hovering around her went back to his post near the door, and we stood and looked at each other in the faintly musty gloom.

She said, "Well, did you see Mr. Fabri?"

"Yes, I saw him. Do you mind telling me what your husband said?"

"Oh dear. It was nothing, really. I think he said he supposed he'd better have a look at you. Something like that. As if you were something he didn't take seriously but had to show an interest in. If— if I hadn't met you, I probably shouldn't have taken any notice. As it was— But mainly I was upset because I thought you must have known who I was. But so long as you didn't—" She looked at me, a very long, uncertain, questioning look. Then she suddenly smiled. "I'm sorry I'm such a fool," she said. "Look, I've written you a formal note asking you to dinner tomorrow. There'll be a bridge four and us two, so we'll be able to talk. You can tell me about Mr. Fabri then. I mustn't stay now. You'll come, won't you?"

"I'll come."

"That's right. I've asked you about bridge—in the note, I mean. Say you don't play, and stick to it. All right?"

"I will, I promise."

She nodded and moved away. I went on with my Edgar Wallace. It seemed a very long way from Kallar Kot. I almost had a mind to buy it, but was fairly certain I should be charged the full price for what was really remainder stock. When I looked up, she had gone. I put the book back among its timeless companions and went out to my car.

CHAPTER

11

THE LAMBERTS' HOUSE WAS IN THE MIDDLE OF THE
old cantonment and more like the old-style English
officer's bungalow than anything I had seen yet. The
garden was neat with a sort of routine neatness.
There were flower pots all along the steps of the
verandah. Only the English flowers were poor speci-
mens. They probably badly needed an injection of
fresh seed from the home nurseries. I was taken in
by a superb creature who wore a long green coat
between his rustling pajamas and his starched white
turban.

Patrick Lambert was an older man than I had expected by quite a bit. He was tall and bull-necked,
with a dark jovial face and a quantity of iron-grey
hair, which he wore rather long. He was a bit of a
dandy altogether. I set him down at sight as an im-
penetrable egotist. He had all the charm that often

goes with it. Mrs. Lambert was nowhere to be seen.

Patrick Lambert looked me up and down, smiling. Even his handshake was tentative. He said, "Hullo, Gilruth. Nice of you to come at such short notice. I thought we ought to have a word, but I gather you've already seen Fabri."

"Yes, I saw him this morning."

He nodded, still smiling. He poured out a thick dark whisky and handed it to me. He took his eyes off me just long enough not to spill the whisky. "Now tell me," he said, "are you a bridge player?"

"I'm afraid not." I assumed an elaborate concern. "I hope you weren't relying on me," I said.

"No, no. We have a four in any case. Come along, then." There was a tall, completely dazzling blonde who could only be a Scandinavian. She was introduced by a Muslim name, but I gathered her husband was not present. She was so like a statue that you did not in any case expect her to speak much, and in fact I heard her say very little the whole evening. Patrick boomed and hovered around her, and she responded with a widening of her grey eyes and an occasional guttural monosyllable. I suppose she was all right at cards, but it must have been a bit like playing bridge with Galatea. The other two were a Pakistani couple of tremendous suavity and charm, the husband a slight, lean man and the wife a flashing, full-blown beauty with a tremendous battery of make-up and a long cigarette holder. She wore the Indian evening dress that has none of the European décolleté but leaves uncovered a ring of brown flesh all around the body at about the level of the midriff. They were a glamorous company altogether. A moment later Mrs. Lambert floated in from whatever she had been doing behind the scenes. She was all in white and radiant as ever. It struck me at some stage of the evening that she and I alone talked English English. Her husband was a wonderful talker, but pure Dublin.

The talk flowed around the social and political fringes of the business of government, but the atmosphere and the social code were cosmopolitan. We might have been in the capital of any one of a dozen small states. Here I was not a ghost at all but a straightforward visiting foreigner. Away to the northwest, Kallar Kot still stood above its empty torrent bed, and no doubt the jackals howled in the dusk from the scrub on the far side. But here the world was neutral, if a little unreal. The whisky lapped me in a familiar peace, and suddenly across the flow of talk I caught Mrs. Lambert's eye and held it for a long, long second. Just before she looked away the radiance clouded, and I thought how much you could love this woman if she was after all a little unhappy. Now I had seen her husband I could imagine reasons why she should not be happy. But I had only now suspected a flaw in the crystal, and the thing might easily be subjective.

The meal was elegantly conducted, but the food

not, in fact, particularly good. The hotels offered Eastern and Western food, neither of them very successfully. Here there was an attempt to marry the two, and the offspring, except in the occasional detail, was undistinguished. There was an unnecessary and unalluring fish course. Patrick Lambert, served last, ate a mouthful slowly and then, during a moment's silence, put his fork down with a small distinct clink on the side of his plate. He and his wife looked at each other down the length of the table. There was nothing to be read in either face. Then he turned with some cheerful blarney to Galatea, who was absorbing hers, as she did everything she was offered to eat or drink, with a placid and elegant thoroughness that I found completely fascinating. The conversation was carried by our host and the Pakistani wife, with adequate support from their opposite numbers. I did what was required of me, but very much from the sidelines. Galatea opened and narrowed her grey eyes and smiled her slow golden smile. It was difficult to tell how much English she really had, but her natural role was clearly not that of a conversationalist. We all got up together and found coffee and the bridge table ready in the next room. The players went to it seriously, as to the main business of the evening. Mrs. Lambert said, "Mr. Gilruth, bring your coffee in here. Then we can talk without upsetting the game."

She led me through a curtained doorway into a

small side room. The Pakistani gave me one urbane, slightly quizzical glance as I followed her. None of the others took the slightest notice. We sat at the opposite ends of a sofa with a small coffee table between us. We could not see the bridge players, nor they us, but the curious staccato conversation of a bridge four formed the background to all we said. She settled herself back into her corner with the quick, unselfconscious movements of a child or an animal making itself comfortable. She still wore Pakistani dress, and sat with one leg slightly drawn up, almost as if she was riding side-saddle. Then she gave me, for the first time that evening, her sudden brilliant smile. She said, "Now tell me what you're supposed to be doing out here."

I looked at her. For the moment I had no thought in my mind but to smile back into her smile, but I had to make up my mind. Finally I said, "I'm not very happy about it, to tell the truth."

"It isn't merely coming back here that's making you unhappy?"

"No," I said, "not only that, certainly." We sat there, both with our heads leaning back against the sofa, looking at each other. The suggestion of unhappiness seemed to change her natural gaiety into an overwhelming gentleness. I said, "Tell me why you think merely coming back here might make me unhappy."

"Well—I don't expect you were very happy out

here, were you?"

"No. All right, I wasn't. But what makes you think so?"

She was twisting her hands together in her lap, and now she looked down at them, as though she was trying to shape what she wanted to say between her slender fingers. "I don't know," she said. "I think—I think people who like trying to run this country are not generally very nice people. I mean the people who actually enjoy it. I don't mean the people who do it because they feel they ought to."

I said, "I think that's true of all countries to some extent."

"Yes, but this one particularly, don't you think? My father was unhappy most of the time. But then it was his own country. To anyone coming from outside, it would have been sort of magnified either way. If you enjoyed it, you enjoyed it more because it wasn't your own country. If you didn't, the fact that it wasn't your country made it worse. Isn't that right?"

She lifted her eyes, and again we looked at each other along the shiny satin of the sofa back. From the next room the Pakistani wife called out in mock horror, "But my God, darling, why did you have to go three hearts on that lot?" There was a burst of laughter from Patrick Lambert, and then the dry, precise voice of the Pakistani explaining what he had meant by his bid. It was all very cheerful and urbane. I felt sure Galatea was opening her eyes at her partner, but she did not make this audible. I said, "How do you know all this?" and she shrugged. It was a very comprehensive, un-English gesture.

"It's my country," she said. "And I did not think you would have been one of the ones who enjoyed trying to run it."

I smiled at her, and she stopped looking worried and smiled back at me. "May I take that as a compliment?" I said.

"Of course," she said. She put out a hand suddenly. Mine went out to meet it, and we touched fingers for a moment. "Dear Mr. Gilruth," she said, "I like you very much."

It would have been conventional at this stage to ask her to call me Jim, but I did not in the least want her to call me Jim. To hear her say "Dear Mr. Gilruth" was an enchantment in itself. I was still wondering how to say what I wanted to say when she sat up suddenly on the front of the sofa and said, "But you still haven't told me what you're supposed to be doing. Only that you don't like it. What is it you don't like?"

I sat up too. For better or worse, I had made my mind up now. I said, "I was brought out here by a body calling themselves Anglo-Pak Enterprises. That was what they called themselves in London, anyway. Is that your husband's concern?"

She looked at her hands again, frowning. "I—I think so. You see—I really know very little about Patrick's professional affairs. He's not secretive, exactly. It's just that he never goes out of his way to tell me anything, and I don't like asking questions. Is that what Mr. Fabri's in?"

"Apparently. At any rate, Mr. Fabri seems to be in charge of the thing I've been brought out for. And I gather your husband's in it too."

"What is it, then, this thing?"

"They have a project for an industrial development at Pind Fazl Shah, in Fazilpur. They brought me out because they thought I might be able to help them get hold of the land they want. I was S.D.O. Pind Fazl Shah for a couple of years not long before I went home. They say the scheme will be a good thing for the whole area. I wish I knew whether it really would. Mr. Fabri's selling me this view of it, naturally. So was one of their people I met in Lahore, only less directly. I assume your husband will too, if he talks to me about it."

"I see that. But I still don't understand what it is they want you to do for them."

"I think they want me to cash in on a moral obligation."

She frowned. "That doesn't sound very nice. This was an obligation that arose when you were S.D.O. there, all those years ago?"

"I think so. I decided a case. It was a criminal

141

case. I decided it as best I could, but I don't think, now, that my decision was just." I realized as I said this that I had not said it to anyone before, even myself. "But of course one party was pleased by it. I think I did it as much as anything to please that party. Now these people want me to get something back on it. Well, all right, if they have the right on their side. But I must know. I don't want to go wrong a second time from the best of motives."

She said nothing for a bit. She sat leaning forward, working her hands together, as she had before, and staring at whatever the invisible stuff was she molded between them. Then she said, "I don't think you ought to let a single imaginary injustice worry you, not after all these years. Even if it was real, it doesn't count for much in the sum total. Injustice is the custom of the country. It happens all the time."

"But it was my job to stop it. What else was I there for?"

"Of course, of course. But it wasn't a dishonest decision, was it? I mean—there was nothing in it for you?"

"I suppose not. I did what I thought was right. Only I'm not sure I got the right answer. And it was my job to do that."

She looked at me. She was smiling slightly now. She was like a patient grown-up arguing with a fractious child. I did not mind in the least. She said,

"Look, Mr. Gilruth. Did you ever, during your time out here, make a deliberately dishonest decision? I mean, you may have bent the law occasionally, but only because you felt that law and justice weren't the same thing. But did you ever intentionally perpetrate a wrong?"

"No. Why should I? I had nothing to gain by it."

"That's it. Very few of you people ever did. You made mistakes, of course. You misunderstood things and were misunderstood yourselves. But according to your lights you were honest. Everyone knows that, whatever they say. I don't say it justified everything you did, but it helped."

"I know that. All the same, this thing happened. And I don't want to make it worse."

"You can't just leave it—contract out, refuse to have anything more to do with it?"

"I don't think so—not yet, anyhow. I suppose there's a nagging idea in my mind that I might do something to put things right. Do you see what I mean? Turn what I did to good account. Anyway, I want to know more about the thing before I decide."

She sighed. "You're hopeless, aren't you?" She thought for a moment. "Would you like me to find out what Patrick really thinks about it, selling apart? He's got no reason to sell it to me."

"Do you think you could? And you could form your own judgment, couldn't you, on what he said?

143

It would mean an awful lot to me."

"All right. I'll try, anyhow. I told you, I don't like asking questions. But I'll find out what I can. May I write to you?"

"Please do," I said. The curtains swayed, and Patrick Lambert came in beaming. "Dummy at last," he said. "Hildi won't play a hand if she can help it, but she couldn't dodge this one. What about a drink, Gilruth?"

"I'd like one," I said. I got up and followed him through into the next room. Galatea, impassive as ever, was gathering in the tricks as methodically as she had her mouthfuls of fish. I wondered—you always do with women like that—what you would have to do to shake her and what would happen when you did.

Patrick Lambert was at my elbow with another dark whisky. "An amazingly beautiful woman," he said. He said it in a light conversational tone, as no one else in the room understood English. No one in fact showed any sign of having heard it.

"Yes," I said, "wonderful."

He turned and wandered back to the drinks table at the far end of the room. He began pouring a drink for himself. He said half over his shoulder, "Are you going to be able to help us in this Fazilpur thing, do you think, now?"

"I don't know. I told Mr. Fabri I'd think about it."

He swung around with his drink in his hand. He was a large, handsome animal and suddenly menacing. He said, "We got you out here in the belief that you could."

I smiled at him with a geniality I did not feel. "I came out to do a survey," I said, and he tossed his big head impatiently.

"Ah, what's the difference?" he said.

He went back to the bridge table, leaving me standing there with my drink. As far as I knew, Mrs. Lambert had not got up from where she was sitting. I hesitated, and then sauntered over to the table. Galatea had made her contract, and Lambert was dealing. The Pakistani wife flashed a bright eye at me from over her cigarette holder. "You don't play this game?" she said.

I shook my head.

"You're wise," she said. She riffled through her cards with expert jeweled fingers, but did not sort them. The smoke from her cigarette drifted across her face despite the long holder, and she squinted at the cards through it. "A spade," she said. "Then you mustn't waste your time watching us. You go back and talk to Subeida. She doesn't play this game either."

Galatea said, "Two hearts." Her voice was deep and hollow. It was as if the statue had suddenly asserted itself. After that, battle was joined and nobody took any more notice of me. I drifted away

145

as casually as I had drifted up and went in through the curtains. Mrs. Lambert was sitting back in her corner, looking at me as I came in. There was very little expression on her face. I put my glass on the table with the empty coffee cups and sat down in my corner of the sofa. She said, "Have you never been married?"

"Not yet," I said. I had thought I wanted to marry Estelle in the early days, but now the subject was not raised. We both of us knew it would not do. I was shaken suddenly with an appalling stab of homesickness for Estelle and Estelle's flat, which was as near a home as I got. It was quite incongruous that I should feel like that, sitting there with that woman who shone with her own warmth, so that you instinctively held out your hands to her. With Estelle you were always waiting, watching for a gap in her defenses or a lowering of her guard. Even when it happened, you never quite knew what the terms of surrender were. All you knew was that it would not last. It was wonderful while it lasted, but you had been warned. To me at least, Mrs. Lambert seemed to have no defenses at all. I do not mean physically, but that did not seem of any great importance. It was the immediate mental intimacy that counted.

She said, "Out here one has to. I mean a woman has to. The nearest I could get to any measure of freedom was to marry a European."

"What freedom does that entail, then?"

"Well—social freedom, obviously. The rules of Muslim society no longer apply to you in the same way. Your individual freedom is a matter of personal adjustment. But whatever freedom your marriage allows you, society can't take it away from you."

We looked at each other, as we had before, along the shiny back of the sofa for what seemed a very long time. I did not put the question, not because I did not think it needed putting, but because I did not think she wanted me to put it. She would tell me, in her own time and her own way, how free she was.

I asked to be excused before the bridge was over, and drove back to the hotel very slowly, with the roof off the car. The whisky had no noticeable physical effect, but blanketed the emotional sensitivities like a layer of foam rubber. Pind Fazl Shah seemed a thousand years ago and a thousand miles away. But I was still a very long way from home.

12

I DO NOT THINK I HAD EVER STAYED AT BHAGRIAN REST House in the old days. It was too close to Pind Fazl Shah to make it worth my while to camp there. Rest houses were what the old books, and perhaps the older provinces, called dak bungalows. The name was inappropriate, because, generally speaking, no one ever went to a rest house unless he had work to do in the neighborhood. Officials on government business used them free. I suppose if a private person got permission to use them, he paid rent of some sort to the Public Works Department, but none of the rest houses I used would ever have ranked as tourist attractions, except one or two pleasantly sited at canal headworks on one of the great rivers.

It had already been arranged that I should go to Bhagrian for a bit, and I saw no reason to change this. If the Subedar-Major wanted to see me, he could find me there easily enough. I had no doubt it would be seen to that he heard I was there. I drove out to the rest house with my suitcase and a roll of bedding, borrowed from the hotel, in the back of the car. Even in the twilight simplicity of British rule you used to move into a rest house with quite a retinue. There were horses (if you were doing your job properly) and grooms, a driver for your car, at least one domestic servant, a clerk or two and a stenographer, and probably a local subordinate officer with his own personal entourage. Now it was only a ghost with his hand baggage. A cook had been laid on by my employers. This did not sound promising, but in fact I ate better at Bhagrian than I ever did at the hotels. I collared the cook as soon as I got in and told him firmly that I would eat only the food of the country. This meant in practice that I lived on chapatis and eggs during the day, with a real curry and pilao in the evening. As ghosts go, I did not do badly at all.

I had written my polite letter to the S.D.O. at Pind Fazl Shah—his named was Akhtar Hussain—telling him what I was doing and saying I hoped to call on him at his headquarters presently. I moved in, settled my things, drank a cup of tea and went out to look around me in the last of the daylight. The spring harvest, which in these parts is almost entirely wheat, was well up and in places beginning to turn. The pale green covered all the buff-colored, uneven country where there was any soil at all to grow it on. Every small field was in fact a cultivation terrace, leveled itself as far as possible but seldom on quite the same level as its neighbor. They were tailored to the natural contours. It had never struck me before how like they were to the Celtic fields of the hill farming of early England. It had rained again, and the air was clear and sweet. Bhagrian village and police station were nearly half a mile away. There was not a soul about. I wandered off across country, following the tracks that joined the main village and the outlying hamlets and occasionally walking along the little earth dykes which separated field from field.

I felt completely alone. It was even slightly disconcerting. Twenty years ago I had never felt alone. I had been the center of too many converging interests to be let out of anybody's sight for long. My presence in the rest house would have been known, and although anyone who had official business with me would have had his say and gone home by this time of the evening, there was always the odd encounter, casual or contrived, with the man who had something on his mind that he did not want to commit to paper or say in front of the clerks. It had been part of the job that you were never wholly free of it. You neglected the infinite heart's ease that private men enjoyed, though you had few of the prerogatives and, unless you were of a particular type of mind, none of the satisfactions of royalty. Now it was different. I did not imagine the system had changed much, not out here among the scattered villages. But I was no longer part of the system. Not that I would be again, not for all the tea in China. As Mrs. Lambert had said, we had done our best according to our lights, but once was enough.

I got back to the rest house in the dusk and found oil lamps burning in the main room. They smelled as they had always smelled. The tall bare room was chilly, and I asked if any wood was available for a fire. Wood was not a thing to be taken for granted in these parts. They said it was, and an old dark-skinned man with a stubble of grey beard brought in an armful of the writhen, thorny sticks that the local trees supplied and then a shovel full of glowing coals to put under them. He knelt and blew on them with the gentle repetitive breath which alone will work charcoal up into a proper heat. The blue fumes added themselves to the smell of the lamps. It was almost unbearably evocative. I watched the old man kneeling and blowing, and suddenly wondered what had become of the blacksmith who had lost his son and his daughter at Kallar Kot, on just such an evening as this, twenty years ago. I did not think he would be still alive. The kindling crackled suddenly, and there was a spurt of flame. I longed for the old man to go away and let me tend the fire for myself, but he still knelt there, nursing it.

I said, "That will do, father. It will be all right now. I'll see to it."

He looked at me doubtfully and again at the fire. He did not really trust me with it. He put two more sticks in position and then said, "Very good," a little regretfully. He piled the spare sticks carefully on each side of the fireplace. Then we exchanged formalities and he left. I pulled up one of the long, cane-bottomed chairs to the fire and sat back in it. The cook appeared in the doorway and asked hopefully if I was ready for supper. I did not want to keep him late, but I wanted to be left alone, if only for a little longer. I said, "After half an hour," and he said, "Very good," exactly as the old man had said it, with a world of resignation. I did not like being worked on like this. I had had too much of it in the past, and I resented it. What was the good of being a ghost if I could not rid myself of even the minor griefs of my previous existence? It was getting the worst of both worlds.

The fire burned up well. Every now and then it let an eddy of blue smoke escape from the side of the chimney. The smoke mixed with the smell of the lamps, as the charcoal fumes had, and the flames threw an orange flicker across their steady yellow glow. I sat there with all the elements of sensuous enjoyment under my hand but full of an endless regretful disquiet. I had, here and now, undeniably come home to what I remembered. There was no more putting it off. Nothing would ever be more familiar than this. But the house was empty. It had nothing to say to me, nor I to it. To remember my old unhappiness did not reconcile me to the present. My old innocence was tarnished by its confrontation with my present self. The worst of both worlds was what, after all, I was going to get, and it was no good being too upset about it. I got up and went to the door. It was quite dark now. There were voices and orange lights in the kitchen across the brick-paved yard. Otherwise there was nothing but the chilly air smelling of crops and wet earth. I shouted for supper. The answering shout was full of relief and enthusiasm. I found suddenly that I was very hungry. There was always food, and then I could sleep, and tomorrow the present might begin to move again.

The food was very good. Everything slowed down, and I gave up the struggle. There was only myself as I was in surroundings which, however clearly I remembered them, were new to my new self and really, when all was said, very pleasant. Only there was still something I ought to be able to do and could not, or something I was looking for that I had not found.

The Subedar-Major came to see me next morning. I did not recognize him nor he me. I suppose I remembered him as a type. A fine specimen of a fine type, but still a typical figure, not an individual.

153

And twenty years had played hell with him. The twenty years between the sixties and the eighties play hell with most people, but I had let myself think of him as timeless. He was still very tall and erect, but he walked laboriously with a stick and one very stiff leg. His sight had nearly gone. Even through his thick, silver-framed glasses he obviously saw very little. The mustache still bristled, but it was sparser and yellowing. And he smelled very slightly. It was not the real stench of dirt and neglect, but the stale musty smell that very old bodies seem to have, whatever you do for them.

He did not really believe it was me. Not, in his case, because he saw the changes in me, though God knows they were there to see, but because he could not bring himself to believe what he had been told. He dragged imself to meet me, but did not at once put out the expected hand. He stood there, peering at me. He said, "Gilroz Sahib?"

It was the first time anyone had called me that for twenty years. Most English names got fixed in a local form as soon as their owner reached the country. The second syllable of my name had been well beyond the country's powers, whereas *roz* was a familiar word. Gilroz sounded in fact very Persian, and I had got rather fond of it. I said, "Yes, Gilroz Sahib. Welcome, Subedar-Major Sahib."

He was still not sure. He said, "Our same Gilroz Sahib who was here before?"

"The same one," I said.

154

Then he put his stick against the table and took my hand in his two leathery old hands. He made an odd little whimpering sound, and I thought for a moment that he was going to weep. But a man like that does not weep easily, even in his eighties. Instead he said, "You have come back to stay?"

"Not to stay," I said. "Just for a little, to see it again."

"Just for a little," he said. He had the trick many very old people have of repeating what he had just heard, as if to make sure he had got it right. He said, "Sahib, those were good times."

I did not take this politically, or even personally. He meant the times when he had been strong and in command of himself, even in his sixties, and had married a young wife and got a son by her. God forbid, I thought, that I shall ever be old enough to look back on my sixties as a good time.

I found an upright chair for him and sat him down on it. I sat down close to him. He did not seem to be at all deaf, but I wanted to be where, so far as he could, he saw me. We made polite inquiries after each other's health. He said, "I am an old man. I walk very slowly. My eyes are bad." He passed his fingers to and fro in front of his glasses, as if to show he hardly saw them. "Still," he said, "I get by." He thought for a moment. "Are you married?" he said. "You were not married when you were here."

I said not.

"What?" he said. "Why have you not married in your own country? Here perhaps it was difficult for a wife. But in your own country you ought to marry."

I wondered what explanation I could give. At home there were half a dozen stock phrases you could use. They did not answer the question, but they dealt with it and left you to your private explanation. Here you could not do that. Partly, I suppose, it was your limited control of the language, but it was also because all speech was simpler and more direct, whoever was speaking it. You found yourself saying things, and meaning them, which you could not say in English without striking an attitude or a false note. I remembered this very well. It accounts for a great deal of what strikes the ignorant as false and ridiculous in English stories about India. Even so, I tried to shrug it off. "I didn't have a mind to marry," I said. "A man works better alone."

"Better alone," he said. "What work do you do, then?"

"I write books."

I knew as I said it that he would not take it well. He said, "Indeed?" with polite interest, but he could not really understand it. He said, "You don't do any government work?"

I shook my head, and for a bit he peered at me, frowning slightly. I had a feeling he was in doubt again whether I was really the same Gilroz Sahib. Finally he said, "But, Sahib, how has this come about? Here the government was in your hands. You were like a king among us. Writing books is all very well, but what sort of work is it for you?"

I said, "Times have changed, Subedar-Major Sahib." He knew that, of course. What I wanted to tell him was that I had changed, or perhaps that the gap between the way he had seen me and the way I was had become unbridgeable. Twenty years before, the gap had been bridgeable, partly because I was different in myself and partly because of the compelling human instinct to be as you are expected to be. You saw it happening all the time, sometimes to the verge of the ridiculous. You saw callow products of the grammar schools and universities, innocent certainly of any instinct of government and suspicious by inheritance of the part they were expected to play, become quite suddenly patriarchal and a little more than life-size under the sheer pressure of public expectation. I suppose the artificial disciplines of the fighting services play on the same instinct.

He said, "Times have changed." Then he smiled suddenly. Dignity had always been, and was still, the keynote of his face, but whereas his smile had used to be full of devilment and charm, it was now unexpectedly ghastly. It was something to do with his teeth and the way his cheeks had fallen in. "I'm too old to change," he said. "You're a young man. You can understand. It is very difficult for me to understand new ways."

"You have a young son," I said, "Akbar Khan. I've met him."

His whole face lit up. "Akbar Khan?" he said. "You've met him?"

"I think so. In Rawalpindi. He was with a friend."

He nodded delightedly. "With a friend," he said. "He is a good boy." He swallowed and then said harshly, "My son older than Akbar was a martyr in the war. Did you hear?"

"I did hear," I said. "I'm sorry."

He made a little brushing-away gesture, as if to put the thought of it away, or perhaps to brush aside my condolences. "He was in the battle at the Bhaini Bridge, on the canal."

I had heard of Bhaini. The Pakistan infantry had counterattacked against fearful odds, throwing back the Indian 15th Division and blunting one of the five prongs pushed out to grasp Lahore. The one thing I wanted to know, I could not ask. And then the Subedar-Major told me. "Mirza Khan," he said. "He was a major. He was a good boy, too." Not Bahadur Khan, Mirza. Whatever had happened to the young man I had discharged, he had not died a hero's death. I looked at the Subedar-Major's hands, folded together in his lap. That was an old person's trick, too. All the time I knew he was looking at me through his thick glasses. I was certain now that we had reached the same thing in our minds, and both knew that it must be left where it was. We were tied together by this thing, but it was something we must not talk about.

I think it was my desperation to find a new subject that made me go straight to the other thing which was in my mind. In any case I did not think that anything but a frontal attack would serve. I said, "They were saying there is a scheme for a big new factory at Pind Fazl Shah."

He came back very sharply on this. "Who said so?"

"Akbar Khan," I said. "He said there were proposals of the sort, but you were against them."

He unclasped his hands. They were trembling slightly, and one of them reached around for his stick where it leaned against the table. I suddenly saw that he was in a fury. Not with me, but with the people, whoever they were, who threatened his whole order of things in a way he could hardly take in.

"Here too," he said. "In Kallar Kot. They want to buy my land."

"And you don't want to sell?"

He was on his feet now, leaning on his stick. I got up too, but he was still half a head taller than I was. His whole face worked with rage and incredulity and a horrifying hint of something like panic. I

159

thought, King Lear in the storm. He said, "Sahib, we are army people and landholders. We do not sell our lands. You know that. These people can do what they like. When I am dead, Akbar Khan can do what he likes. He is a young man. I am not selling."

He calmed down before he left. I promised to go and see him at Kallar Kot, but half his mind was still on the other thing. There was a man waiting for him with a small gaunt pony. I did not want to see the painful business of mounting. We said good-bye and I went back into the rest house. I was shaken with unhappiness and a kind of chilly revulsion which I was ashamed of but could not overcome. But even before I got inside the door I had decided that I must speak to Akbar Khan.

13

I CALLED ON THE S.D.O. AT THE PROPER TIME OF THE morning and with due notice. He used the same, rather cramped office room as I had used. It was probably even the same table, only this time I sat on the visitor's side. I got a small perverse satisfaction out of this reversal of roles. There was a touch of suspicion, almost hostility, in the way he received me. I did not blame him for this, because I had been less than ingenuous with him when we first met. In any case, it did not worry me. He said, "So you have an interest in this development project?"

I did not like his choice of words, though I thought it very probably unintentional. I said, "Well—not a personal interest. They asked me to come out here because they thought I might be able to help them. I don't think I can, in fact, but that seems to have been their idea."

"I see. In what way could you help them?"

I thought he probably knew, and in any case I saw no need to prevaricate now that I was clearer in my own mind. I said, "I expect you know Subedar-Major Fazl Dad Khan of Kallar Kot?"

"Of course. I have met him two or three times." He betrayed no great enthusiasm.

"When I was S.D.O. here I made a decision in a criminal case. The Subedar-Major felt indebted to me for this decision. That was not why I made it, of course." I did not at all like telling this small, quick man about the Kallar Kot case. It would all be ancient history to him, but his mere sitting where he now sat somehow laid my defenses open.

He said again, "Of course. What was this case?"

"A son of his was arrested in a murder case. I took the committal proceedings here and discharged the accused for lack of evidence. I think if I had committed him he would have been acquitted in the Sessions Court anyhow. But of course the Subedar-Major did not want him tried."

"I see, yes. But I am not clear what connection there can be between this and what is going on now."

I smiled at him, trying to melt his suspicion. "To be honest," I said, "Nor am I. When I came out here, in fact, I had forgotten all about the case. It was twenty years ago, after all. But since I have been here, I have begun to understand what I think these people have in mind. The Subedar-Major is threatening to hold up their project. They thought I might be able to persuade him not to."

He made a little swallowing noise in his throat. I think in fact it was merely a trick of hesitancy, while he was wondering what to say, but it gave me a faint preliminary stab of irritation. Then he said, "That does not seem very probable, perhaps." I had already said so myself, but I did not like hearing him say it. It seemed to cheapen something, if only an illusion I no longer held. But my annoyance was much too unreasonable to be allowed to appear.

"I certainly haven't made any attempt to persuade him so far," I said. "I have met him—he came out to see me at Bhagrian. I know he is strongly opposed to the scheme, but I don't think I really know the rights and wrongs of it."

I do not think he had been listening to this. His eyes had wandered out through the dusty wire gauze of the window at his side. "You say you discharged his son in a murder case. Which son was it?"

"I wanted to ask you about that. I have met the Subedar-Major's youngest son, Akbar Khan, and I know another, Mirza Khan, was killed in the September war. The one I discharged was called Bahadur Khan. What became of him? Is he still alive?"

He was looking at me again now. I did not much like his expression. There was a touch of amusement in the small, intelligent eyes that made me un-comfortable. He nodded. "Oh yes," he said. "Baha-dur Khan is still alive. He lives at Dhok Saidan. But I have not met him." He looked out of the window again. "I did not know he had been accused in a murder case," he said.

"It was all a very long time ago, after all."

"Yes. Well, that's where he is now. Dhok Saidan is not far from Kallar Kot. It is part of the revenue estate, of course. You could go and see him, per-haps, if you wished. Have you met any more of your old acquaintances? There is a senior member of the bar, Mian Mohammad Ibrahim, who says he remembers you, but he does not practice much now."

We went on to talk of things as they had been and as they were now. I did not take to him. There were too many things he knew which I had not and things he did not seem to be interested in which I remembered thinking important. He had a curiously world-weary air, as if the whole business of govern-ment was something to be got through but not a matter for personal involvement. When I got up to go, I said, "What about this project, then? Is it a good thing?"

He half smiled and shrugged. "It will come, I think," he said. But he was neutral. That was the extraordinary thing. He spoke as if it was next year's monsoon, which he merely took cognizance of. I could not know when and in what circumstances I should see the S.D.O. again. I suppose it would not have made any difference if I had. The lack of sympathy was instinctive and inevitable, and the whole relation bedeviled by a sort of jealousy, across a gap of twenty years, over the one thing we had in common and took different views of. We parted, on this occasion, with polite formalities. On the only other occasion we met, politeness was neither here nor there and the formalities were of a different kind.

I do not know why it was now inevitable that I should go and find Bahadur Khan. I think it was because he seemed to be an unknown factor in a calculation that I was still trying to make. I had at some point to talk to the Subedar-Major again, and I had made up my mind to talk to Akbar Khan. I wanted to see Bahadur Khan before I did either, and that whether or not they knew I had seen him and he was mentioned between us. If he was not a factor of any significance, I could at least exclude him from the calculation. If he was, I could not deal properly with either of them until I knew where his significance lay.

The only alternative was to do what Mrs. Lambert had suggested and pull out of the thing altogether. I have been over this in my mind again and again, but I still cannot see that it could have done any good if I had, except perhaps to my own peace of mind. The thing would have gone the same way in the end. The lines were already laid down. My intervention, so far as I intervened, was useless, but no worse. Anyhow, I was not at that time ready to pull out, and I therefore set about finding Bahadur Khan.

Dhok Saidan was, as the S.D.O. had said, an outlying hamlet of Kallar Kot. I walked the last couple of miles to it, unaccompanied and unannounced, on an afternoon when the cloud had suddenly cleared and the sun come out in that startling strength which always, at this time of the year, reminded you suddenly of what it was going to do later. Every year or so, I found, you forgot what the heat was really going to be like until these sharp reminders brought you face to face with it all over again.

The first sight of Dhok Saidan was unimpressive, and a nearer view did not improve it. The houses were all of mud brick. There was no rock or natural height here, only the slight mound of mud and refuse heaps with the flat shapes of the houses growing out of them like rectangular fungi. There were not more than four or five of them. After the rain the whole place smelled sour. The sun was drawing out the exhalations of accumulated neglect, but had not yet had time to dry it up and sterilize it. The path ran in on a curve under the thin shade of the acacia trees, making for a narrow gap between the houses. There was a milch buffalo tethered to a tree and a bunch of boys playing tip-cat on the bare earth between the edge of the crops and the foot of the mound. They stopped and stared at me as I came up, looking me over with faintly derisive incredulity. Then the small bright boy who lurks at the back of every bunch of boys emerged from the ruck. He came out on to the path and gave me a military salute. He said, "Good day, sair." This did not of course mean that he knew I was English. I was foreign, and English was the foreigner's language. I returned his salute solemnly and said, "Good day." After that they all tried it until I got tired of it. I said in their own language, "This is Dhok Saidan?" and then, when they agreed in concert, "Does a Bahadur Khan live here?"

They all fell silent, looking from one to the other and wiggling their bare toes in the dust. Then the bright boy said, "Yes, sir, he lives here." He nodded towards the bunch of silent houses. I said, "Will you show me where?" He said, "Come on," and then, as they had before, the others all joined in, saying, "I'll show you" and "This way, sir."

I went on up the path with the boys milling and giggling just ahead of me. A girl of ten or eleven, with a naked baby astride her hip in the crook of one arm, came out of the gap and stood there. She looked at us for a moment and then turned and darted back between the houses. The lane was barely wide enough for two people to pass. A noi-

some drain meandered down the middle of it, fed
with grey fluids from under the walls of the houses.
I had been in many such places, but I would not
have associated one with a member of the Subedar-
Major's family. The boys swarmed and chattered
ahead of me, and the flies flew up in clouds out of
the drain and crawled on the sweat of my face and
head however much I tried to beat them off. An
ownerless dog, dreadful with the mange, slept
spread-eagled across the lane in the sun. When he
heard us coming, he opened one eye and for a moment watched us over the side of his head without
moving. Then one of the boys made a gesture of
throwing something at him, and he got up and
slithered off down the lane with his hairless tail
between his hairless legs. He did not make a sound.

At the top of the mound the lane branched to the
right, and just beyond that there was an open doorway in the left-hand wall. Like all the others, it
led into a small open courtyard with the doors of a
single-story house beyond. The boys said, "This is
it." Then they stood back in bunches on both sides
of the doorway, waiting to see what I as going to do.
There was an element of amusement in their curiosity. Their eyes reminded me of Akhtar Hussain's
eyes when I asked him about Bahadur Khan. I
thanked them and told them to go, but they took no
notice and hung back, smirking. They had a right to
be where they were, and I could do nothing about

it. I ignored them and stepped through the doorway into the courtyard.

I want to be careful about this. Of course the courtyard and the whole dwelling were primitive by Western standards—the open mud hearth, with the cow-dung cakes smoldering under the blackened pot, the open drain running out under the wall, the up-ended string beds with their bedding hung out on them, the water stored in earthen pitchers. But places of that sort can shine with housewifely pride, like the raddled and polished doorstep of a sooty terrace house. I have seen it over and over again. There is always something touching and comforting in it. But this place was sordid as well as primitive. The air in the sun-filled yard was noticeably fouler than the air in the lane outside, so that you checked at it as you went in and tried to keep your mouth shut. There was loose debris on the plastered floor and flies busy on things that should not have been there at all.

A woman crouched with her back to me, working on something with her hands. I saluted her respectfully and asked if Bahadur Khan was at home. She turned slowly and looked at me over her shoulder. She was not particularly old, but hard-faced and rather thin. She said, "Yes," but did not move. Then from inside the house a man's voice called, "Who is it?"

The woman said, "I don't know. Someone's

come." There was the creaking of a string bed inside the house and a man appeared suddenly in the doorway. He held on to both doorposts with his hands, and his eyes blinked in the sunlight. He was bareheaded. The henna dye was growing away from the roots of his short grey hair. He had no beard or mustache, but several days' bristle. He looked at me with his red-rimmed eyes fluttering and his mouth not quite shut. I had no doubt he smelled terrible, but I kept my distance. I had really seen all I needed to see, but a sort of horrible anger drove me on, and I could not let it alone. I gave him an elaborate salute and greeted him by name. He turned and dived into the house, and reappeared a moment later pulling an untidy turban on to his head. His eyes were all over the place. He said, "I don't understand. Who are you?" His voice was very hoarse and high. The hands that fiddled with his turban were tremoulous and very thin. He looked twice my age.

I said, "Gilroz Sahib. I discharged you in the murder case."

He made a noise between a giggle and a whimper and said, "Gilroz Sahib? I did not know you. You have come back?"

"Certainly I've come back," I said. "I gave you a chance twenty years ago, Bahadur Khan. I have come back to see what you have made of it."

This was all quite unjustifiable and quite untrue.

It was myself I was lashing, not this poor junky who had never done me any harm beyond getting himself indicted for murder in my court. He had given me a chance, and I had come back after twenty years to see what I had made of it. Only this was not what I had said.

I said, "You didn't go into the army?"

"No," he said, "no, I'm a farmer." The woman still squatted there with her head turned over her shoulder, and I knew the boys were still clustered outside the doorway. This was the Subedar-Major's eldest son. There was no primogeniture, it was true, but also there was no disinheritance, not of land. The surviving half-brothers would inherit equally when the Subedar-Major died. He was looking around now, gathering together the shreds of his gentility, wondering whether to ask me to sit down, but by now I had had enough. I said, "Well, I must go. Good-bye, Bahadur Khan." I spoke gently, but I could not bring myself to touch him.

He pulled one hand away from the doorpost long enough to return my salute, and then I was out of the doorway, with the boys, silent and pop-eyed, hanging back on either side. I went off along the lane, avoiding the black slime of the gutter, and down between the steaming refuse heaps to the head of the field path. One of the boys ran up alongside me and said, "Sir, where have you come from?" I said, "Bhagrian," and he repeated, "Bhagrian" and

171

dropped back, none the wiser, to tell the others. Out among the fields the sun was very fierce now, but I was in a mood to welcome discomfort. You could never work these things out. If Bahadur Khan had been hanged twenty years ago, I knew he would have lived on in his father's memory as an ornament of the army, a good boy, like his brother and half-brother. Who was I to weigh the loss of a hero against the gradual recognition of a degenerate? Only so far as I was concerned there was one thing less to be said for myself, and I had needed more.

I did not know whether the Subedar-Major would hear of my visit to Dhok Saidan. I did not think he would hear of it from Bahadur Khan. But I could not face him now until I had talked to Akbar Khan, and Akbar Khan was in Rawalpindi, not out at Pind Fazl Shah. It was time I got back. Even out there, among the sun-struck fields, I quickened my pace.

14

MRS. LAMBERT RANG UP NEXT MORNING. SHE SAID, "How was Fazilpur?"

"Well—a bit worrying, to tell the truth."

"I'm sorry," she said. "Look. Patrick's in Dacca. Will you come and see me? I can tell you a little about this business, I think. That is, if you still want to know."

"I suppose so. Yes, I'm sure I do. Anyway, I want to come and see you."

"Oh dear," she said. "I don't know if it's very wise. But come, all the same. Come in about an hour's time. Ask for Patrick. Then when they say he's not in, ask for me. I'll give you coffee. Would you like that?"

She spoke, as she had spoken to me before, as if she was comforting a lost child. I wanted the comfort too badly to worry about the incongruousness of it.

"I'd like it very much," I said.

"All right. You come, then."

The man with the green coat must have gone with his master, but a lesser servant showed me in. She was sitting in the same corner of the same sofa. We went through the formalities, and she sent the servant for coffee. I said, "Do your servants understand English?"

"Not this one. Haider does quite a bit, but he's gone with Patrick." She shook her head at me suddenly. "But even this one's not blind," she said. "You mustn't look at me like that. I mean—not when he's in the room. Otherwise I don't think I mind. So long as you don't do it to everybody."

"I didn't know I was doing it. But I'm glad you don't mind."

She sat up. "Mr. Gilruth, let's be sensible. I'll tell you about this Pind Fazl Shah thing. Then you can be looking intelligent when he brings the coffee. You understand I can't give you a very coherent picture, because I couldn't ask too many questions. I—I don't think Patrick liked my asking, as it was."

"I'm sorry. Well?"

"Well—first, it's very big. They are big people and the project is a big one. There's a lot of money involved. But it's purely a private thing. There's no state backing—not yet, anyhow. The idea is to get the project on to a fairly firm footing first. Then I said wouldn't a thing like this turn Pind Fazl Shah upside down? It was a pretty primitive part, and so on. Patrick had no doubts on that at all. He said a jolly good thing if it did. Of course, there'd be people who wouldn't have things as much their own way as they had at present, but for the great majority a development like this must mean more money and more security all along the line." She thought for a moment. Then she said, "Mind you, that's Patrick's point of view. It's bound to be. He's an engineer. He doesn't—" She moved her head from side to side while she groped for words. It was one of her entirely un-English gestures that went so oddly and so charmingly with her very English speech. "He doesn't know very much about this country, you see, not really. I mean, he doesn't have to. His problems are technical ones. The social effects mean nothing to him. Why should they? All the same—he does know what this will mean in purely physical terms. And granted that—well, then I suppose it depends on your point of view. Any big change of this sort makes trouble somewhere, obviously."

I said, "You know the country. It's your country. And these things have happened in your part of it."

"Yes. Yes, well, I think it's got to come here, too. They haven't got the canals up here. And you can't bolster an uncertain agriculture entirely with army service, even when we're building up the army as fast as we are now."

I nodded and said nothing. I must have looked worried, because she said, "And that's not what you wanted to hear, is it? I'm sorry. I don't seem to be much comfort to you."

She really was sorry. Gentleness and concern poured out of her, and she put out a hand to me. Then the coffee cups rattled on the saucers beyond the curtains, and by the time the tray appeared coyly through the gap I was sitting straight and watching it. She bent to pour out the coffee, and when the man had gone we sat facing each other over our cups, consciously the richer for something that had not happened.

She said, "What went wrong in Fazilpur? Can you tell me?"

"Nothing worse, I suppose, than an ordinary process of disillusionment. But I admit it upset me."

"The same old case?"

"The same old case, yes."

"Still convicting yourself of injustice?"

"Not so much that. Only that what I did, just or unjust, seems to have been pretty completely useless."

She put her cup down with a defiant bang. "Mr. Gilruth," she said, "it's no good. Worrying about an old injustice is bad enough. Worrying because something you did was useless is worse. How many of the things one does will stand up to that sort of test twenty years later? Even the most deliberate

176

decisions. Even in our private lives. I've made a big enough mess of things, if that's any comfort to you."

She got up and walked to the doorway. I put my cup down and followed her, but she turned around and came back to me. For a moment we just stood there. Then she put her hands on my shoulders and kissed me, very gently. "Now I think you'd better go," she said. "What are you going to have to do next?"

"See people." I thought for a moment. "Do you know a Major Nazir Ahmad?" I said.

"What—the one Patrick calls the Galloping Major—more English than the English—calls everybody old man?"

"That would be him, all right."

"What on earth do you want to see him for?"

"I don't. But I want to see a junior officer in the same regiment. A boy called Akbar Khan. He comes from Pind Fazl Shah way. Only I don't know where to find him."

"I can tell you that, if he's the same regiment." She told me where the mess was. It was a bit complicated, and I scribbled notes on the back of an envelope. She said, "When shall I see you again? I shall see you, shan't I?"

"You will. I don't know when. I don't know what my movements will be. But I think I'm reaching the point of decision."

"And when you have decided?"

177

"Then I'll go home. What else is there to do?"

She looked away from me and nodded. "You're quite right," she said. "One always goes home in the end. There's nothing else to do." We touched hands. There did not seem to be anything else that needed saying. I went back to the hotel and wrote a note to Akbar Khan asking him to come and see me. I found the mess at last, but not Akbar Khan. I left the note and went back to the hotel to wait for him.

He came early in the evening. He was a little puzzled and hesitant, but nothing could obscure his natural grace and good manners. He said, "Mr. Gilruth? I remember meeting you, of course, when I was with Nazir Ahmad. But I hadn't really cottoned on to who you were. It was the name, partly. You must be the great Gilroz Sahib of Pind Fazl Shah that my father's always talked of."

He smiled, of course, as he said it, but there was no mockery in the smile. In so far as the thing was a joke, it was a joke I shared with him. We sat down in the dun-colored dusty armchairs with the low round table between us. He looked at me with friendly curiosity. "Well," he said, "what can I do for Gilroz Sahib?"

"I had to talk to you," I said. "I was out at Bhagrian the other day and saw your father. But first, can I take you up on one point? You say your father's always talked of me. Talked how and to whom?" He smiled again, and I said, "The thing

178

really is important. Put it like this. Has your father said things which might suggest—I don't know, perhaps to someone who didn't know him particularly well—that he really would let himself be influenced by my judgment in any particular case? Do you see what I mean?"

"Oh yes. Mirza and I— Mirza was my brother. He was a good deal older than me, but we always got on."

I nodded.

"Well, Mirza and I always felt that for my father you somehow personified the good old days. Do you know what I mean? There was a colonel of his, too, he was always talking of, but he's been dead some time. We never really knew—I'm sorry, this must sound rather rude, but you'll understand—we never quite knew how far you were a real person, if you see what I mean, and how far you just stood for something in my father's mind. But there's no question that from the way he talked any other person might think that you were the ultimate authority on almost anything. Especially if the person didn't know the old man as well as we did. He's an obstinate man really, you know. It's never been much good trying to argue with him." He stopped and sat there, looking at me. He radiated good humor. "Does that help?" he said.

"Yes. Thank you. It helps quite a lot. I think I had better tell you the whole story, hadn't I? That is, as far as I know it."

"I think it would be better, yes, if you don't mind."

"Well—I was at Pind Fazl Shah—oh, before you were born, I should think. Your brother Mirza must have been a boy. At any rate, I don't think I ever met him. Your father was a good friend of mine and of course a pillar of the administration—you can understand that." He nodded. I thought he looked a little apprehensive now, but I had to go on. "You had—you have—an eldest brother, Bahadur Khan. Now look, Akbar Khan—I've seen Bahadur. I went and saw him the other day. I know he's no good, and I don't expect you're very proud of him. But he comes into the story. He got mixed up in a murder case. He came up before me. The evidence wasn't strong, and I discharged him. I—I had your father very much in mind when I did that. It would be that, chiefly, that would account for his attitude, don't you see? He was pretty desperately concerned at the time, naturally."

He looked very solemn. "So that was it," he said. "Poor old Bahadur. I knew there was something, but not quite the whole story. That explains quite a lot, in fact. A murder case, was there?" All of a sudden he seemed unbearably young, like all the solemn subalterns who went gravely to their deaths because it was the grown-up thing to do. He said, "He's a very sick man, you know, Bahadur."

180

"I know that. I've seen people before who looked like that. Anyway, I'd better finish the story, if you haven't already guessed how it ends. There are these people with their development scheme. You said something about it the other day. I don't know how far you realize it, but your father's holding them up. They can't compel him to sell them the land they want—not legally, anyhow. They got me out here, ostensibly for some sort of survey, but in fact in the hope—on the chance, anyway—that I might persuade your father to do what they want. I've only recently understood this. Now I've seen your father. I know his attitude and I didn't attempt to persuade him. Now I've seen Bahadur, I know he doesn't really count. So I wanted to talk to you about it. I hope you don't mind."

He was frowning ferociously, not at me, but at something in his own mind. I thought anger was not a thing he was used to and it did not suit him. Whatever it was in his mind that made him angry, he did not speak about it. Instead he said, "What do you think about this project yourself?"

"I can't pretend to a proper knowledge of it. I've found out what I could. On balance I think probably for everyone's sake it ought to go ahead. On the other hand, I understand your father's feelings. I feel a bit the same way myself. But then I'm a relic of the old times, too."

"Yes, well, I feel much the same. So far as I'm

181

concerned, I should be inclined to give these people what they want and let the thing go ahead. But I'm damned if I'm going to have my father made to do anything he doesn't want to. He's getting on a bit, after all. He doesn't think as clearly as he did, and a thing like that could be the death of him." He thought for a moment. "I tell you what," he said, "it's time I went out and saw the old man in any case. Suppose we go out to Kallar Kot together one of these days and have a talk with him? What do you think?"

"I think that would be admirable, if you can spare the time."

He said, "Right, we'll do that." He was quite grown-up again, and curiously decisive.

I said, "Look, Akbar Khan, there's one thing you must understand. I hold no brief for these people. You know that, don't you? They got me out here pretty well on false pretenses, and I'm not playing their game for them. In so far as I favor the scheme, I favor it as a matter of independent judgment."

He was all warmth at once, desperately anxious to show that there was no misunderstanding. "Of course, of course," he said. "I suppose it was worth their while to try. It must strike you, doesn't it, that they are very well informed?"

"That has always struck me, right from the start even, when I first saw them in London."

"Yes, well they have their—their local contacts,

damn them. I'll tell you about that some time, perhaps. It all joins on, I fancy. I hadn't realized quite
how much, in fact." He got up. "Right," he said.
"I'll fix things with Kallar Kot and let you know.
You're free any time, more or less?"

"Any time. That's what I'm here for. I'm at your
disposal."

He nodded. "I'll let you know, then." He raised
his hand in a gesture that had more of the village
than the cantonment about it. Then he was off
across the hotel compound in quick, springy steps.
His movements were the youngest thing about him.
I watched him out of sight with a desperate but
unreasonable apprehension. The Subedar-Major was
an old man, almost out of reach. We had not re-
established any real contact. But this boy was so
nice, so nice. I did not like the way things were
going.

I got up and went outside. It was dusk now. I
wanted some air and exercise, or I should not sleep.
The plum-colored Volkswagen went down the
road just as I came to the hotel gate. I saw it only
after it was past, and never got a sight of the driver.
It reminded me of Mr. Aziz before it occurred to
me that it might in fact be him. There were no
doubt other plum-colored beetles, and I had not
noticed his number. All the same, I wondered.

15

THE WEATHER WAS GREY AGAIN WHEN I SET OUT WITH Akbar Khan to drive to Kallar Kot. I wonder, looking back, how far my memory is colored by the fact that throughout the whole affair the sunshine was no more than intermittent, as it is in England. Characteristically, the landscape of the northwest Punjab is flooded all day with pale red-gold light. The water-colorists used to say that you had to cover your white paper with a red-gold wash before you started to paint, or your tones would remain hopelessly cold. That was how I remembered it. It was pure chance that I ran into a spell of spring rains, with cloudy skies and grey landscapes, but I have no doubt it magnified for me the sort of desolation I found myself in and the sense of time lost.

We used Akbar Khan's car. It was bigger than my Morris, and he was used to the rather rough road beyond Pind Fazl Shah. The hotel gates were partially blocked by a trap driver having trouble with his horse. The two-wheel trap was loaded with six passengers, three facing forward and three backward. The driver, when he got started, would sit on the step. But the lank pony could not or would not shift the load, and was plunging desperately between the shafts while the driver, half crouched on the tarmac, hacked at its legs with the wooden handle of his whip. The passengers, muffled in their homespun cloaks, sat in impassive irritation, like railway passengers when the train is late starting. They had their own troubles, and the torment of the plunging beast meant nothing to them.

Akbar Khan edged his car around the obstruction and drove on. His face was expressionless. You always had, in the long run, to put the local treatment of animals out of your mind, and over the years you got better at it. But I did not know, now, whether to let the thing lie between us or ease my mind, and reassure myself on our relation, by putting it into words. In fact it was he who made the move. "These people are very ignorant," he said. He looked straight ahead, his face revealing neither anger nor embarrassment. He merely stated the fact.

I said, "I think they live so near the borderline themselves, they haven't much concern to spare for suffering elsewhere." It was what I had always told myself, to turn aside my own helpless anger from the people who did these things. It seemed funny that I should be defending the country's unconscious brutalities against the censure of a man who had been born and brought up among them.

He seemed to feel this. He turned and gave me a quick sideways glance. He said, "Perhaps that's it. But it is very bad."

He turned his mind to the road again, and we went on into the dark, rugged country. He drove as I did, or as I thought I did. It had never occurred to me before how much driving was an expression of a whole attitude of mind, even a culture. The curious thing about most Pakistani drivers was that, although they seemed in my judgment to do rash and perverse things, they drove much slower than people did at home. Their whole attitude suggested a lack of sympathy and understanding between them and the vehicles they drove. They sat back and controlled, across a measurable mental gap and without much confidence, an alien piece of machinery. At home even the learner driver identified himself with his car almost from the start; the car had become part of the human organism. Akbar Khan, too, drove fast and by subconscious reflexes rather than by conscious calculation. Something of the Western habit of mind, which was so clearly marked in the make-up of the army, came through in the way he handled the car. He did not, like the Galloping Major, talk Sandhurst English, but he drove his car, quite unconsciously, English-fashion.

He drove in silence for quite a long time. Then he said, "I've been thinking. I think we must persuade my father, if we can, to accept this thing. I am afraid what may happen if he doesn't. He is an old man, and I can't be out at Kallar Kot very much, even from Pindi. And I might be posted away any time." It was the matter-of-fact way he said it that made the thing so suddenly chilling.

I said, "What do you think might happen?"

He took some time to answer this. I thought that once or twice he started to speak but thought better of it. Then he said, "You see, there is a lot involved in this. A lot of money, of course, but more than that. There is a question of honor, too—of *izzat*, you know?" He used the Urdu word which he had already translated as honor, but which carried a whole range of overtones. "For my father, selling his land means giving up his whole position in the village—in the district, I suppose. There are people who would be glad to see him do that. People with old grudges. Well, you have worked out here. You must know the kind of thing, eh, Gilroz Sahib?" He turned and gave me a quick smile, but the smile was for me only. He was not smiling at the thing he had in mind.

I knew, of course. The isolation, the timeless dwelling on wrongs, which even in an English village could mean families which stood apart for generations and relatives who, year in, year out, did not speak. Only here it was something more like eighteenth-century Scotland than twentieth-century England. He said, "Some of these people, I tell you, they're regular bastards." It was the sort of phrase the Galloping Major might have used, but Akbar Khan was in deadly earnest.

I remembered the look on the Subedar-Major's face when he had said, "These people can do what they like." There had been defiance in it, but a startling lack of assurance. I said, "Surely your father's in a very strong position." But I knew as I said it that I was asking to be reassured rather than trying to reassure him. For the first time since I had come back, I suddenly regretted my long-lost authority. Or rather, not my personal authority, but a residuary presence of power which at least thought and operated basically as I did, the friend of my friend, the enemy of mine enemy. I did not like to think of that stubborn, upright, almost blind old man at the mercy of new powers he did not trust and only partially understood.

Akbar Khan gave me a quick, doubtful look. "He's all right legally, of course. But money talks, you know, these days." He sighed suddenly. I thought, he's out of his depth, too. All he wants is to get the thing settled and go back to the life he understands. And then it struck me as odd that life should be so much simpler for a commissioned officer in Rawalpindi Cantonment than for a land-owner's son in Kallar Kot.

I wondered about the succession. I said, "Was Mirza married?"

He had no doubt about my train of thought. He said, "Yes, but he had no son. Only two little girls." He hesitated and then gave me the missing piece without my asking for it. "And Bahadur's got no children," he said. "I'm not married, of course."

That was it, then. One stubborn old man who could not last long, one poor cipher who might die even before his father, and this boy, who would marry and have sons, but was not married yet. I did not pursue the matter, but I liked it even less.

When we went through Pind Fazl Shah, the machinery of government had still not packed up for the day. The muffled figures still sat around under the lowering sky, waiting. The petition writers were still at their desks under the trees. Uniformed policemen came and went. Akbar Khan drove slowly through it, with quick sideways glances here and there. He said, "The seat of government. Really, you know. For us, I mean."

"Still?" I said. I meant still after twenty years, but I knew that he did not remember it twenty years ago.

"Oh yes," he said. "In fact, more than ever, I think, under the present set-up. There's this concentration of authority, you see. The local officers

have more responsibility than ever, and there's less
control from the top. At least, there's very little
political counterweight to the executive. The old
political machinery has been dismantled. Well, it
had to be, it wasn't doing any good. But there's
nothing yet in its place. It puts a great strain on the
executive services, naturally."

"Too much?" I said.

"In some cases, yes."

It seemed ridiculous, after twenty years, that I
should hesitate to ask about the present S.D.O. Yet
I did hesitate. I did not want Akbar Khan, with his
smiling deference to Gilroz Sahib, to suspect me of
wanting to play comparisons. Whether or not he
guessed which way my mind was working, he gave
me the lead himself. He said, "You've met Akhtar
Hussain, have you?"

"Yes," I said, "twice."

He nodded. "I don't know anything against him,"
he said. "Not for certain. I can't say I find him very
impressive myself."

I said, "The worst thing I know about him is that
he doesn't particularly like your father. Well—I
suppose I don't know even that. But that was certainly my impression."

He gave me the ghost of a smile. "That's very
probably my father's fault," he said. "All the same,
I think it's a pity. You never know when it mightn't
pay you to have the local authorities on your side."

The road plunged into the rough country south of Pind Fazl Shah. We went a lot slower now, climbing the ridges in third and dropping down into the steep little valleys, all at different angles and none of them holding any one course for long. Seen from the air, the country would no doubt make sense as a watershed, the rough hills cut by a branching pattern of drainage lines. On the ground it was chaos. The grey light had dwindled into an early dusk, and even with the car open your sense of direction gave way altogether under the perpetual writhing of the road. At last the road plunged downwards more sharply, and I suddenly knew where we were.

The low water-worn cliffs hung over the road, with their fringe of thorn trees dark against the narrowing strip of dark sky. There was not a flicker of movement anywhere. The bloodless vegetation clung to its precarious foothold, as though a breath of air blowing between the enclosing walls would dislodge it. Below the road, the hillside plunged steeply to the bottom of the gorge. If we had stopped the car, the silence would have been absollute, but it was a detestable place, and I did not want to stop in it. Akbar Khan drove a little crouched over the wheel, lifting his head every now and then to look at the darkness above us. I think he also felt the menace of the place, though it must have been familiar ground to him. When the road ran out at

191

last into the river bed, he sat back and took first one hand and then the other off the wheel, flexing them as if to relax the muscles after too long and hard a grip. There were one or two yellow lights already showing in the grey, piled-up outline ahead. We bumped over the culvert and began to climb up among the houses of Kallar Kot.

A lot of people watched us arrive. They stood silent and muffled in the dusk, in lamplit doorways or on the flat roofs of the houses. Some raised a hand in greeting, others merely watched. One figure I remember stood all by itself on the roof of a small house. It stood with its arms folded across its chest, clutching its homespun mantle around itself. Nothing showed but the clutching hands and the eyes, which stood out darkly above the fold of cloth taken across mouth and nose. It did not move at all; only the staring eyes followed the car as it moved past in the street below. After a bit the car could get no further. Akbar Khan turned it into the gateway of a wide courtyard with two oil lamps burning on the walls. We got out stiffly and stretched ourselves, and servants came and took our baggage. He said, "We'll walk up to the house, if you don't mind. There isn't really room for a car."

"Of course," I said. He exchanged a few words with the people in the yard. Then he gestured me ahead through the gateway, and we walked up the slight hill in silence. It was almost dark now. The village smelled as villages in the dusk had always smelled, of woodsmoke and cooking and tobacco, of paraffin fumes from lanterns and the reek of the burning dung-cakes, which burn like peat and have as characteristic a smell. Twenty years ago, if I had come with a shooting party or on a family occasion, I should have felt at home and wonderfully at peace here. Now I went silently by Akbar Khan's side, not knowing what was going to come of it.

The Subedar-Major met us in the courtyard of the house, beaming from behind his thick glasses. He held out a hand to Akbar Khan, who took it between both of his and bent his head over it for a moment while they murmured greetings. Then I found my outstretched hand grasped, as it had been at Bhagrian, by the two old hands, and the Subedar-Major, babbling a little with pleasure and excitement, led us into the house. My room on the upper floor was Spartan bare and spotlessly clean. There were army group photographs on the walls. I wondered if it had not been Mirza's room before he was married and perhaps later when he came, as Akbar had come, to visit the old man from wherever he was serving at the time.

We washed and reassembled downstairs for a meal which not even my mental oppression could prevent me from enjoying. The Subedar-Major was in high spirits and did most of the talking. His talk was almost wholly of the past, as it is with most very old people, but it was vivid and full of zest. It was the present he could not face. When later, over cigarettes and tea, Akbar Khan tried to bring his mind back to it, he was suddenly full of the protective evasiveness that makes the old so exasperating to deal with. Akbar Khan would say, "Gilroz Sahib and I have been discussing this—" or "Gilroz Sahib and I agree—" and the old man would peer from one to the other of us with a sort of querulous indignation, as if we were combining against him. We were, after all, the two people he had counted on most for support, and he could not understand how our views could differ from his.

Whatever we said, it always came back to the same thing. The land was for Akbar Khan. When the Subedar-Major was dead, his son could do what he liked with it, but the old man would not, in his son's lifetime, alienate his son's birthright. Akbar Khan's protests that he wanted the land sold were smiled on and disregarded, as if he was a child who did not know any better. Bahadur was never mentioned. It was no good going on. The old man was getting querulous and upset, and we were getting nowhere. He sat there in his straight, high-backed chair, staring straight in front of him. "Never," he said, "never, never, never." For the second time I thought of King Lear. Another old man who did not know what he was up against.

I was tired and went to my room once I saw it

was no use. I did not sleep for a long time. The floors were single boards laid on joists, and the voices came up from below, not quite intelligible but very audible. Father and son, old father and young son, talked for an hour or more after I left them. They went, I think, out of the formal Urdu into the language of the district. I did not think they were arguing now. They were discussing something very earnestly—at times, I thought, with deliberately lowered voices.

The whole atmosphere of the place weighed on me. Akbar Khan's return to his village had too plainly not been that of the well-regarded young squire. There were the retainers and adherents, and there were the others. The thing was medieval but also, to me, familiar. I had been in villages like this before, villages split from top to bottom into irreconcilable factions which permeated and distorted everything. Kallar Kot had not been one of them. But now the Subedar-Major's old paramountcy had gone, and I smelled faction in the air. I did not know how it influenced or was influenced by attitudes to the development project, but I knew enough to be certain that in this, as in everything else, the parties would range themselves on opposite sides. It was not only the Subedar-Major against the developers. It was the Subedar-Major against the people who wanted the thing to go ahead. Regular bastards, Akbar Khan had said. So they might be. Violence was native to the place, contained or merely dormant, but always there.

Next day the sun shone and the apprehensions of the night seemed a little unreal. But they had left their mark on all of us. Akbar Khan carried it off with something of his natural gaiety, but nothing came very easily. We did not mention the thing at all, but it was in all our minds. We left the Subedar-Major standing in his courtyard, and as we went down the hill to the car, I heard the clatter as the wooden doors shut between him and the street. We went down, as we had come up, in silence, and during the whole of the journey back we had next to nothing to say to each other. Akbar Khan stopped the car at the hotel gate and we both got out.

"Well?" he said.

I shook my head. "I don't know. I'll have to go and see these people. But there's nothing much else I can do, is there?"

"I don't think so." He held out a hand. "You've been very kind," he said.

"I was very fond of your father in the old days."

"Yes. But I don't think he'd have listened to you even then—not on this."

"I agree," I said.

"Anyway," he said, "thank you for trying, Gilroz Sahib." There was no smile with it this time. We shook hands solemnly. He was one of the nicest young men I have ever met.

16

I THINK MR. FABRI WAS WAITING FOR ME. THE MAP I had seen before was in front of him on his desk. It looked to me as if the red hatching had spread further since then, but that may have been my imagination. There was certainly not much left unhatched now between the black dotted lines except for the great gap in Kallar Kot. He said, "Well, Mr. Gilruth, I understand you have been out to Bhagrian and also, I believe, to Kallar Kot. And you have seen Fazl Dad Khan. I wonder what you have to tell us?"

"Nothing much, I'm afraid. I have, as you say, seen the Subedar-Major twice. I have also talked to his son, Akbar Khan. On the second occasion we saw the Subedar-Major together. He is quite determined not to sell."

Mr. Fabri said nothing for a moment. Then a door

behind him opened and Patrick Lambert came in and stood behind his desk. The two of them just looked at me. Their faces were quite expressionless. "For what it's worth," I said, "I may say I myself think your plans ought to go ahead. So far your decision to bring me out here was justified. But I'm afraid you were wrong in believing that I might be able to influence the Subedar-Major." Mr. Fabri nodded slightly, but nobody said anything. I said, "I don't know whose idea it was that I might. I gather you have your local sources of information. It may not in fact have been wholly unreasonable of them to expect the Subedar-Major to listen to me, but unfortunately they were wrong, whoever they are. I am sorry to have put you to all this trouble and expense."

Patrick Lambert folded his arms across his chest and leaned back against the wall. His great head was lowered, watching me. Mr. Fabri went on talking to me as if Lambert was not there. I did not know which of them was the boss man. I found it very unnerving.

Mr. Fabri said very slowly and distinctly, "I do not think any apology is called for from you, Mr. Gilruth. As you say, we seem to have been misinformed. I myself always had my doubts. Now they are confirmed.

He sat silent for some time. There was nothing more for me to say, and I simply waited. At last he said, "Can you tell me what Fazl Dad's reasons are? In so far as he has any. It may be mere obstinacy."

"He is obstinate, of course. He is a very old man. But for him this is very much a question of honor. It means everything to him to keep his land. In particular, to keep it intact for his son to inherit."

"For Akbar Khan? I understand there is another son living."

"For Akbar, yes. The other son is of no significance."

"You say you have seen Akbar Khan. What is his attitude?"

"The same as mine. He is not against this project. The Subedar-Major knows this. But even this does not seem to influence him. So long as Akbar Khan is there to succeed him, he will not sell."

He nodded. "I see," he said, "I see. I am grateful to you for making the position clear."

I said, "There seems to be nothing more I can do, and I should not put you to any more expense. If you agree, I will make arrangements to go home."

Patrick Lambert spoke suddenly. He did not raise his head, but went on looking at me from under his thick dark brows. "You've been a bloody washout, Mr. Gilruth," he said. "Can't you think of something to shift the old bastard? It's got to be done, you know."

I said, "The Subedar-Major is a friend of mine. It's not my business to force his hand. Incidentally,

199

it's not what I was hired for."

He threw his head up with a jerk, as he had once before. It was a very animal gesture, like an angry bull. He said, "Ah, you have too many friends in this country."

For a moment we stared at each other. Then I turned to Mr. Fabri. "What do you propose to do next?" I said.

He still did not seem to know Patrick Lambert was there. He smiled, almost indulgently. "The project, of course, goes forward," he said. "There is still a great deal of work to be done. This—" he waved his stubby white forefinger casually at the map— "this is a minor problem, after all. It will no doubt settle itself. Such problems do, I find. But, as you say, it is no concern of yours." He got up. Nobody said anything more, and there was nothing more I could do. I simply bowed myself out. I never saw either of them again.

I went to the P.I.A. office and made a booking to fly home in three days' time. I wanted a day or two more here. I could not quite make up my mind that the thing was at an end so far as I was concerned. I did not particularly want to see Lahore again, so I would wait the three days in Rawalpindi and then fly home in one piece. I had to see Mrs. Lambert again. I had told her I should, and in a part of my mind I very much wanted to. But not for the moment. I had to get rid of the other thing first.

I went back to my room and sat in my usual chair, looking at the empty chair where Akbar Khan had sat. I wondered if he would come and dine with me. It might not do any good, but I could not just let the thing go, and he was the only sane contact I had with it. I rang the mess, but he was not available. I resigned myself to an empty evening, and began to wonder what I was doing hanging on here at all. Then, just as it was starting to get dark, the wire door of my room was swung back and Mr. Aziz walked in on me, unannounced.

I did not get up. I pointed to the chair opposite me, but he stood there, between me and the door, looking down at me. I think it was the first time he had looked directly at me without smiling. His mouth was drawn down in an almost comically doleful line. He looked like a small boy trying not to cry, but I did not think this meant much. He was certainly bursting with some sort of emotion, but I could not quite tell what. He said, "So you have told Mr. Fabri that Subedar-Major Sahib will not agree?"

"I've told Mr. Fabri the truth," I said. "What else could I do? I'm sorry if your idea didn't come off. It was your idea that I should be brought out to persuade the Subedar-Major, wasn't it? It has cost the company quite a lot of money. I suppose you're not very popular at present, is that it?"

I think it was his expression that made me gibe

at him like this. But there was something that exasperated me, now, in the way the whole thing had been done. It was full of a sort of precocious ingenuity which I certainly could not associate with Mr. Fabri.

He plumped himself down in the opposite chair. He said, "No, but you see—" He sat there, leaning forward, with his hands clasped between his knees, struggling for words. He no longer had his shiny briefcase, and was wearing something much drabber than the blue suit he had sported in Lahore.

"You see," he said, "always Subedar-Major Sahib was saying that Gilroz Sahib would do this and Gilroz Sahib thinks that. It was common knowledge. People laughed at him for it. So I thought perhaps if you considered the project a good one, and told him so, he would agree."

I said, "I do think the project a good one, and I did tell the Subedar-Major so. But he will not agree. I don't see why he should take my word for it when he feels as strongly as he does about it."

"But you were his patron and benefactor. You had done him this great service. I thought—"

"Mr. Aziz," I said, "what great service had I done the Subedar-Major that he was bound to me for in this way?"

He sat back in his chair now, with his square brown hands resting on the arms. He had got rid of his disappointment and indignation, and was suddenly much more formidable. Even his English had improved. I guessed that he had come straight to me in a fury after a stormy meeting with Mr. Fabri. Now the effects were beginning to wear off, and his natural intelligence was in control again. He said, "You let his son go in the murder case. He was guilty. If he had not been the Subedar-Major's son, you would not have let him go. Was this nothing?"

"I discharged Bahadur Khan because there was not enough evidence to support a conviction. It was a perfectly correct decision. He may have been guilty. I don't know. But it could not have been proved against him."

He said, "But you see, Mr. Gilruth, I know he was guilty."

"You know?"

"Of course. Perhaps you have forgotten the name of the old man, the blacksmith, whose girl was taken and whose son was killed?"

"I have, yes. I have tried to remember it, but I can't. I remember the man himself."

"His name was Nathu. The boy who was killed was called Faizu. We all had this sort of name because we were only menials, not pakka Musulman, like the Awans. I was called Zizu. Perhaps you remember now? I told you the truth, but you did not believe me."

I remembered him, of course, now. The dark, intent, enigmatic face of the small boy in court. It

was the same face that looked at me from the opposite chair. It was not, at the moment, all that
changed. It was still enigmatic, with the same hint
of mockery or malice in it. I said, "I see. What happened to your father? I never saw him again."

"He died. He did not wish—he was too unhappy
to live, I think. He died quite soon after. My
mother was dead. It was my sister who had looked
after us, and she was gone. And Faizu was dead, so
I was alone, you see."

I ignored the solitary small boy and kept my
mind on Mr. Aziz of Lahore, with his flashing smile
and his bright blue suit and his plum-colored Volkswagen. I said, "You seem to have done very well for
yourself, nevertheless."

"Oh yes. I was taken to the mission school in
Pindi here. I was clever, you see. I learnt English
and passed my matric, and then I went to college
and learnt engineering. I was a blacksmith, after all.
We had always been blacksmiths. It is not so different, perhaps, once you have been educated."

The part of my mind which was looking for escape routes said, "Nineteenth-century England
again. The blacksmith become ironmaster." But I
said nothing aloud, only nodded.

"So then," he said, "when I heard of this project,
I went to the company and offered my services. I
was working in Karachi then. They like to have
local people working for them. It helps, you see.

204

And of course I had the qualifications. But really I wanted to go back to Kallar Kot. I wanted to see what the Awans would do when Zizu's campany began taking their lands. Of course, the case was a long time ago. Many people had forgotten. But Subedar-Major Sahib remembered. He knew who I was and what I had come for. He started to be a bit scared. I talked to all the other people. They were ready to sell after a bit. The company is offering a good price, of course. So gradually the other people in the village turned against Subedar-Major Sahib because they thought he wanted to keep the village poor when it could be rich. That is what I told them, you see. It is true, of course. You know that yourself. I told them Subedar-Major Sahib wants to keep the village poor, as it has always been, so that he can still be sitting on top of it. And I told the company that the village would force Subedar-Major to sell. But the company said we cannot have force, he must be persuaded. So after a bit I said no one can persuade him except perhaps Gilroz Sahib. If you bring Gilroz Sahib out from England, perhaps he can do it. And so you came out, but still Subedar-Major Sahib won't listen."

He was talking quite quietly now, in full control of himself, but in deadly earnest. I found him very frightening. I said, "Look, Mr. Aziz, it's no good saying I'm sorry about your brother's death. I am, of course. I was at the time. And I am sorry about your father's death. But does it do any good to go on chewing on it like this? It's all a very long time ago. You haven't suffered much by it yourself. The contrary, in fact. You are, or will be, a richer man than the Subedar-Major. If your father and brother had lived, you might still be blacksmith of Kallar Kot. Has that occurred to you?"

He said, "Mr. Gilruth, I want justice. You did not give my father justice. Now I want it."

"You don't want justice," I said, "you want revenge."

He smiled. It was not at all the beaming smile I had seen before. He showed his white teeth in his dark face, but the expression of the face was quite different. "Why not?" he said. "It is the custom here. You know that. Or is it only the landholders who can take vengeance for their wrongs? Perhaps it is not a part of the menials' rights." He paused. He was not smiling now. He ran his pink tongue suddenly around his lips. He said, "You don't understand, Mr. Gilruth. I was a very young boy. I saw my brother killed. I saw the spear go into his belly and the guts come out. Do you think I can forget that after only twenty years? Of course I want justice. You can call it revenge if you like. I do not mind what you call it."

"It was Bahadur who did the wrong," I said. "You do not mention him."

"Bahadur? Bahadur is nothing. You know that.

You have seen him. It is not Bahadur who is doing this now."

We sat there looking at each other for a bit. I was not at all sure he was properly sane. But that had probably been so for quite a time. There was something driving him now, or I did not think he would have talked as he had. I said, "You've just seen Mr. Fabri, haven't you?"

"I have seen him, yes. He told me what you had said."

"And what else did he tell you?"

He shrugged, but his eyes flickered away from mine. I thought he was already beginning to regret having said as much as he had and he would be off soon. He said, "He told me the project would go on." He got up, as I had expected he would.

I said, "I think he told you it was up to you to get a settlement in Kallar Kot."

He had been backing towards the door, but now he stopped and stood quite still. "Mr. Fabri," he said, "has always left it to me to handle things in Kallar Kot. That is my job."

"And now you are required to get results?"

"Results?" He shrugged again. "I think—I think the thing will be settled."

He moved to the door and I got up. I said, "Look, Mr. Aziz. Look at it like this. The original injustice, if you choose to see it like that, was mine. I made the decision. I was a foreigner in your country. But the foreigners no longer have power here. These people are your countrymen, of your religion. They—"

He smiled, almost gaily, and shook his head. "Oh no," he said. "No, you don't understand. These people are Musulmans. I am a Christian, Mr. Gilruth, the same as you are."

I went to the telephone as soon as he had gone and rang the mess. After a good deal of polite inquiry, the man on duty said no, Lieutentant Akbar Khan was still not available. I wondered what message I could leave that would convey anything of the desperate urgency I felt. Then I said, "Is Major Nazir Ahmad available?" The man said he would inquire. I waited, with the receiver to my ear, looking out through the window at the darkening sky. Then a voice said, "Hullo?" Even that was a work of art.

I said, "Major Nazir Ahmad? It's Gilruth here. You remember we met—"

"Of course," he said. "Hullo. Good evening to you. What can I do for you, eh?"

"I must get hold of Akbar Khan," I said. "It's really very urgent. I was out at his village with him last night, and something has arisen of the utmost importance. Could you please, if you can find him, tell him I want to see him as soon as he can manage it?"

"Surely. I'll do that, of course. Yes, he told me you'd been out to visit his father. Grand old boy, isn't he?"

"Yes," I said. "But look, Nazir Ahmad, you do understand? This really is vital."

"Of course, of course." He sounded a little huffed, but I thought he could be relied on. "If he isn't in tonight, I'll see him first thing in the morning. Bound to. And I'll tell him, don't you worry. Nothing wrong, I hope?"

"I—I don't know, you see. There could be, very wrong. Anyway, I'll wait here till I see him."

"Right-oh. You do that." We exchanged courtesies and I rang off. I had done what I could, but I did not know whether it was enough.

17

NOTHING HAPPENED THAT NIGHT OR FOR MOST OF NEXT morning. I had just made up my mind to telephone the mess again when the phone rang. I picked up the receiver and said, "Akbar Khan? Gilruth here." There was a moment's silence and then Mrs. Lambert's voice said, "Oh dear. It's not Akbar Khan, I'm afraid. Are you going to be disappointed?"

I said, "Not disappointed, no. I was expecting him to come and see me, in fact, not telephone. But I thought it might be him."

There was another slight pause. Then she said, "When is he coming to see you, do you know?"

"No. I've asked him to come and see me as soon as he can."

"I see. Look. Patrick's gone back to Dacca, and I've got to go down and join him. I'm going this afternoon. I don't know when I shall be back. I wondered— I don't think Akbar's likely to be able to get in to see you this morning, is he?"

I stood there with the receiver in my hand balancing irrationalities. I admit I am on the defensive about this, but I still think that what I did was not unreasonable. It did not seem likely that I should ever see Mrs. Lambert again if I did not see her now. I had no very logical explanation why I wanted to see Akbar Khan so urgently, or what I thought was to be gained by it. So far as appeared probable, he already knew pretty well as much as I did what he was up against. In the end I brought up a moral obligation in support of what I wanted to do. I had promised Mrs. Lambert that I should see her again, and I knew she would be hurt and disappointed if I did not. All this is the unraveling and rationalization of a few moments of mental turmoil. It must have been, in fact, a few moments, because Mrs. Lambert said, "Mr. Gilruth? Are you still there? Look, I don't want—" The voice was hurt and slightly desperate, and she was not a woman to play hurt for effect.

I said, "I'm sorry. I was thinking. I want to see you very much. It's only that I was worried about this other thing. No, I agree he's not likely to be able to get in this morning. Anyhow, I'll leave a note in case he does. When may I come to you?"

"Any time. You'd better walk in. There's no one on duty."

"I'll be round as soon as I've written a note for Akbar."

She said, "Very well," and put the receiver down.

I got out writing things and then could not decide how much to say. Finally I wrote, "I have seen Aziz again, and now know who he is. I want most urgently to discuss this with you. If you call while I am out, please leave a note saying when and where I can get in touch with you." I sealed the envelope, addressed it to Lieut. Akbar Khan and propped it up on the center table. Then I went out to the car.

There was nobody about in the over-neat compound or lurking dutifully in the verandah. I pushed the door open and walked into the silent house. I shut the door behind me, quietly, because I somehow felt that quiet was called for, and went through into the small room behind the curtained doorway. She was sitting there, watching my face as I came in. She had a half-smile on her lips, but her eyes were very watchful and anxious. I thought she had put her dignity very much at stake, and her dignity was immensely important to her. I did what I did instinctively, because I wanted above all not to seem insensible of this. It would no doubt have looked very ridiculous to a detached observer, but then so would a great many things which people do only for each other. I put the small table carefully on one side and knelt at her feet.

She held out her hands to me, and I took them in

both of mine. She said, "You're very worried. What's the trouble?" It was little more than a whisper in the big empty house.

I said, "The same business. I think it's dangerous."

She frowned with sudden apprehension. "Not to you?" she said.

"Not to me, no. I'm only on the sidelines. But I was worried, yes."

"Thank you for coming, then."

I shook my head, but could find nothing to say. She took her hands out of mine and put them on my shoulders. Then she bent forward and kissed me, but when I wanted to take hold of her, she held me still at arms' length. She said, "I am really quite a bit in love with you, but I don't want you to make love to me. Do you mind?"

"No," I said. "Yes, of course I do. But I'd much rather that you loved me and we didn't make love than that we made love without your loving me."

She smiled her sudden radiant smile. "What a complicated sentence," she said. "But I like it. I think you had better get up. There is no one in the house, and it was nice of you to kneel to me just at that moment. You understand things very well, don't you? But I don't think you had better stay there. Shall I get us some coffee?"

"I don't want you to go away," I said.

"Then come and help me." We went through to a little pantry behind the dining room. The coffee things were all ready. She switched on an electric kettle. She said, "What can you do about this thing?"

"Very little. Only make sure that the danger is understood. Very likely it already is. But I must be sure."

"And then you can leave it alone and go. Please, please, please leave it alone," she said.

"I'm going to. I'm going home in three days' time."

She put her hand to her face like a suddenly dismayed child. She said, "Oh dear. As soon as that?"

I nodded. "That's why I had to see you," I said. "I'll be gone by the time you get back."

She said, "Tell me about your life at home." I told her about things as best I could, but not about Estelle. We carried the coffee back to the small room and I put the table back in position for it. We talked and drank the coffee. There was nothing whatever to look forward to, and this made a sort of timeless peace between us.

When I was going she said, "Has it done any good your coming out here? To you, I mean."

"I don't know—not yet. I suppose I shall be able to tell when I've been at home for a bit."

She nodded. "Please try not to let things out here upset you. It doesn't do."

"I know. I'll try."

"Very well. Off you go, then." We kissed, for the

third time, very lightly and then I went out and shut the door behind me. I got into the car and looked at my watch. It was nearly a quarter past one. A wave of guilt and apprehension flowed over me. I drove as fast as I could back to the hotel, knowing all the time that this was useless and silly. I left the car and almost ran into my room. Nothing had changed. The letter was still propped, unopened, on the table. I picked it up and tore it in half. It was a gesture of pure relief. Then the telephone rang.

I ran to it and whipped up the receiver. "Gilruth," I said.

It was the Galloping Major. He said, "There you are at last. Been trying to get hold of you at intervals half the morning. You been out?"

"Yes."

"I see." He paused, but decided to let it go. "Well, look, it's like this. Akbar had a telegram this morning. From Bhagrian. There's a telegraph office there. From the old man, I imagine. Anyway, asking him to come out as soon as possible. So he's got special leave and gone. He tried to phone you before he went, but he couldn't get any reply. So he asked me to let you know. As I say, I've been phoning you at intervals, but I've only just caught you."

An immensely cold and heavy weight settled in the pit of my stomach. I said, "When did he go?"

215

"Oh—I'd say an hour and a half ago. No, less than that. An hour, perhaps."

"All right. Thank you for ringing. Sorry I wasn't here earlier."

"Yes. I was surprised, I must say. Well, anyhow —you've got the position now."

"Yes, thank you."

"Right-oh, then. Good-bye."

I said good-bye and ran straight out back to the car. I had not really pushed the Morris before, and I must say she went very well. The main roads, as they always had been, were a mixture of straight clear runs and appalling and incalculable hazards. They were getting the cane crop in from the plots with well irrigation, and at places the single ribbon of tarmac was blocked completely by a train of bullock carts, piled high with the long jointed stalks and swinging cumbrously from side to side as the beasts plodded forward under their towering loads. The maneuverability of a loaded bullock cart is very limited, and you cannot hurry it at all. The only thing was to edge past on the unmetaled shoulder, and this, apart from the ordinary hazards of overtaking, meant reducing speed drastically. I stopped twice at petrol stations. Each time I inquired for Akbar Khan's car, but I knew they would not have remembered it unless it had stopped there too. The first inquiry drew blank. At the second pump the man said the car had stopped, but was quite uncertain when. He thought perhaps a couple of hours earlier.

I knew it could not be as much as this. Nazir Ahmad's estimate of Akbar's start had been a considered one. Admitting that he might be driving under the pressure of some anxiety, I did not believe, from what I had seen of his car and his driving, that Akbar could be gaining on me. Whether I was gaining much on him was another matter. At this stage I was not sure what I was trying to do except get to him as soon as possible. It was only later that I was consciously anxious to head him off before he reached Kallar Kot at all. This depended entirely on his stopping for long enough to give me the chance. Most people break a drive of this length at some point. I thought it he had left in a hurry during the morning, he might stop to eat. I went through the familiar stages of hunger myself, but had no intention of stopping anywhere for longer than could be helped. My mental agitation burned itself out as my physical exhaustion increased. An hour before I reached Pind Fazl Shah, I had little left in my mind but the need to get the car on over the increasingly difficult road.

Pind Fazl Shah, so far as the sub-divisional headquarters went, was deserted. I was running an hour or more later than when I had last come through here, and business had ended for the day. There was a single policeman at the road junction just before

the bazar. As I slowed for the turn, I asked him if
he had seen Akbar Khan's car go through. Unbelievably, he answered with no hesitation at all. Yes,
he had seen it.

"When?" I said.

He said, "Just now," jerking his head towards
the Kallar Kot road as if he could still follow the car
with his eyes. I felt a surge of hope and relief, illog-
ically strong because of my nervous exhaustion. I
thought if I could only catch up with Akbar Khan,
I could unload my disquiet on to him. I thought I
knew what his reaction would be. He would smile,
cheerfully but a little grimly, and talk about these
bastards and how we could deal with them. I
whipped the Morris off along the uneven tarmac.
After a few miles, when the tarmac ended, I could
begin watching for the dust cloud ahead. Only now
the light was starting to go, and it might not be easy
to see.

In the end I never saw the car on the road ahead
of me. I knew it was there. I even smelled it. The
evening was dead still, and if I had stopped my car,
I should probably have heard it. It was when I was
well into the broken country before Kallar Kot that
I ran suddenly into a cloud of dust hanging in the
motionless air between the rock walls and smelled, as
well as the smell of the dust, a whiff of petrol exhaust. It could not be very far ahead.

I was very tired now. I had driven myself over

this road only once since the old days, and I had to concentrate grimly on getting the car around the bends and up and down the steep gradients. I knew where I was suddenly, as I had last time, when the road ran out on to a straight shelf and gathered itself for its plunge down towards the river bed. I also knew, at the same moment, that I could not catch Akbar Khan now before he reached Kallar Kot. I might be there only a matter of minutes after him, but I could not stop him going there.

There was still a glimmer of daylight up here, but below me on my left the road went zig-zagging down into almost total darkness. I realized I did not know where the light switches were. I took my foot off the accelerator and let the car run gently forward over the level stretch while I bent forward to find them. After the rush of air and the perpetual noise of the engine, the silence was startling. I was still fiddling for the switches when I heard two shots down in the gorge. They were fired in quick succession, and the echoes took them up and threw the sound up and down the bare walls. Then there was the roar of a car engine spinning in neutral. It roared for a moment at full throttle, and then the sound was merged in a dreadful toppling crash. There were two smaller crashes and then silence.

I had enough control to bring the car to a halt and cut the engine, but I felt desperately sick. I got out of the car and bent down, holding on to the side of it, until the blood came back into my head. As I straightened up I saw the orange light of a fire down in the darkness. The flames were hidden in the bottom of the gorge, but the light danced among huge moving shadows in the clefts and hollows of the cliff. I left the car where it was and began running down the road. As is always the way with a road you have only driven over, I was surprised how far it was and how long it took me on foot. I had still not seen the flames, but all the time the orange light came and went on the cliff face, and after a bit I could hear the roar and crackle of the fire. I was running sharp downhill. It was no great tax on my wind, but the going was rough and in the darkness I was lucky not to fall or turn an ankle. I was not far above the fire when it suddenly occurred to me to be careful.

I dropped to a walk. The roar of the fire was loud now, and as I came around a bend I knew that here, just ahead of me, the car had run off the road and dived into the bottom of the gorge. The lip showed hard against the glow of the fire, and there was a gap in the line of boulders that marked the edge of the road. Then a figure scrambled down from the cliff on to the road, and I stopped and flung myself back into cover. I saw him first in silhouette against the upward glow of the fire. Then he went to the edge of the road and stood there looking down. I could really see him quite clearly. Even if I had not already known who he was, I should have recognized him. He had a rifle in his hand and a delighted smile on his face. I did not in the least want to attract his attention. Without taking his eyes off the fire he worked the bolt of his rifle, and a brass empty leaped out and fell with a tinkle on to the road behind him. I did not doubt that he now had another live round in the breech. I wondered if he would bother to pick up the empty. He did, but not until he had seen all he wanted of what was going on down below. Then he made a gesture with his free hand, as if he was taking leave of what was down in the bottom of the gorge. It was a jaunty sort of gesture. He was still very pleased with himself. He stooped, picked up the empty shell and dropped it into his pocket. Then he set off down the road towards the river bed and Kallar Kot.

The fire was already dying down when I went to the edge and looked over. The shattered carcass of the car was still recognizable. The metal glowed red and the fumes still poured up in the column of hot air, but there was no wind to keep the fire alive. Quite soon there would be nothing but red embers, and before morning nothing but black debris. I did not think there would be anything else likely to be at all identifiable.

I left it and walked back up the road. I had no reason to go to Kallar Kot now. I backed the car with infinite caution on the narrow road and went back the way I had come. At Bhagrian the wicket in the door of the police station was still open and there was a light inside. I went in, and a constable scrambled hastily to his feet and jammed his uniform turban on his head. I stood just inside the door, screwing up my eyes at the light. I suppose I must have looked in a bit of a state, because the man peered at me anxiously. He said, "Sir, is anything wrong?"

I said, "I have come to report a case of murder."

CHAPTER

18

THE POLICE PROSECUTOR SAID, "THANK YOU, SIR" AND
sat down to his papers. I caught Mr. Jinnah's gimlet
eye, and wondered why he wore such a high collar.
I was sure no one else had worn collars like that in
my day. I concluded that the picture must have
been an old one, selected at Partition to perpetuate
the Founder as he had been at some chosen point in
his career. The magistrate lifted an eyebrow at
defense counsel, who got up to cross-examine.

The courtroom was the same, but after twenty
years there had been changes in the casting. Akhtar
Hussain sat in the magistrate's chair behind the table
on the dais. He was smooth, competent and sure of
himself, giving nothing away. I was in the witness
box. Zizu was in the dock. I could no longer see his
toes, but I did not think he had room to wiggle them
inside his shiny winkle-pickers. I doubted if he

wanted to. He too was very sure of himself. He had been on bail from the start. Mr. Jinnah had replaced the King-Emperor on the wall behind the dais. Superficially this seemed the least important of the changes, but this may not have been entirely correct. Only the Subedar-Major was still in place, taking no part in the proceedings, but upright at the back of the court; and he had aged more than twenty years in the time.

Defense counsel was an advocate of the Lahore High court brought over from Rawalpindi. He was a small, courtly man with a grey square-cut Muslim beard, a long black coat and a shining white turban. I had known several like him in the old days. Now he looked rather old-fashioned. But he brought an aura of intense respectability to the defense of bloody, treacherous and lunatic murder. Everything was respectable. Everyone went gravely through the motions and said all the proper things, and I did not believe any of it. I did not suppose I was alone in knowing the truth, but I was made to feel very much alone in stating it. Defense counsel bowed gravely to the court and gave me a sort of respectful, almost regretful, little nod. He said, "Sir, I shall not have many questions to ask this witness." We were all talking English. I had offered to give evidence in Urdu, but as all the people concerned, including the accused, were English-speakers, the court had decided otherwise. I did not like this. It emphasized my outlandishness. In just this respect I was a special type of witness and by just this amount the easier to discount as perhaps mistaken or even prejudiced. Nor did I like the fact that counsel was not going to ask me many questions. If he had any sense, he would leave everything else and interest himself solely in the question of recognition. I thought he had a great deal of sense and would do exactly that. I had waited in Rawalpindi for ten days while the police rushed their investigation through and the Sub-Divisional Magistrate found a special date for the committal proceedings. It had been a bad ten days, and now at the end of it I was not going to be asked very many questions. Equally, this was what, after ten days, I expected.

I had stayed on at the hotel and continued to use the company's car. I proposed to charge everything in due course to expenses. Admittedly they had not in the first place retained me to give evidence of murder against one of their staff, but equally it was not of my choosing that I was going to. I had seen no one except, once, the Galloping Major. He had dropped in one evening and talked with a mixture of sympathy and reproach that I found extraordinarily touching. "Seems such a pity," he said, "seems such a pity." I thought he meant that if I had not been out that morning when Akbar had got the wire, things would not have happened as they had. I believed this too, but I did not let myself believe that Akbar would have been any less dead because of it. I thought I should have been dead with him. There would have been two burned bodies in the car at the bottom of the gorge, and one of them would not have had the luck to be shot at the wheel first. Then the thing would have been written off as an accident. I did not see this would have made it any better, except perhaps for Mr. Aziz and the company he worked for. "I mean," the Major had said, "if he'd bought it in action, that wouldn't have been so bad. I mean, that's what we're there for. But this— I don't know." Civil death was something he found genuinely shocking. Several of his friends had been burned in their shot-up vehicles in those few bitter miles between Amritsar and Lahore, but they were martyrs and, more important, men with a professional aptitude for death. Akbar had died in a sports jacket defending nothing. It was this that seemed such a pity. I liked the Major more than I ever had, but his visit had not made my ten days' wait easier to endure.

The advocate finished rustling his papers and looked up with a small deprecating smile. He said, "How well did you know the accused?"

"During my present visit to this country I had seen him three times before the night when Lieutenant Akbar Khan was killed."

"Three times. I see. And not for long, I think?"

"On the first occasion for several hours. On the

other two only a matter of minutes."

"But you say you would recognize him in all circumstances?"

"Yes, I think so."

"You did not see him at Kallar Kot when you went there?"

"At Kallar Kot? No."

"It would surprise you to know that he was there and that you saw him but did not recognize him?"

"I don't know. It depends on the circumstances. At that time I did not know he was a Kallar Kot man and I wasn't expecting to see him there."

"But you were expecting to see him on the night when the unfortunate accident occurred?"

I should have seen this coming. It made me angry and I counterattacked. "There was nothing accidental about Lieutenant Akbar Khan's death," I said. But there was only my word for it, and I knew it. No rifle had been found, and there was no evidence that Mr. Aziz had ever had one. He certainly had no license to possess one. I knew as well as anyone that as near the frontier as this a very serviceable imitation Lee-Enfield was always to be had at a price, but it was no good my saying so. And there was nothing left in the wreckage to carry a demonstrable bullet wound.

The advocate made a sort of tutting sound, very quietly, as if he was dealing with a fractious child. He was much better than he looked. He said, "Yes, well—that of course is what the court has to decide. But on the evening in question you were expecting to see the accused?"

"No."

"But, Mr. Gilruth, you must excuse me. You said just now—" I said, "May I explain? I was not expecting to see the accused that evening. But when I knew that someone had shot Lieutenant Akbar Khan, I thought it would be the accused. I have already explained why."

"I see. So when you say you saw a man on the road after the accident, you were expecting it to be the accused?"

I considered this, but there were no two ways about it. "Yes," I said, "I was."

"And you did not confirm this expectation by speaking to him?"

"No. I have already said why."

"Yes. Thank you. Now—it was quite dark by then?"

"Yes. But there was the light of the burning car."

"Yes, yes. But there was no daylight or moonlight. Only the light of the fire?"

"Yes."

"And the fire was down in the bottom of the gulley, below the road?" He made an affectation of looking through his notes, though he had the figure in his head. "Nearly thirty feet below?" he said.

"Yes, but the light was very bright. I had seen it

from the top of the hill where I left my car."

"What sort of a light? Can you describe it?"

"The sort of light a fierce fire gives. A yellow light moving as the flames moved."

"A yellow, flickering light?"

"All right, yes."

"And this man you say you saw was standing on the road, thirty feet above it? His face would be in shadow?"

"Only at first. He went to the edge and looked down. Then the light was on his face."

"This yellow, flickering light?"

"The light of the fire."

He sighed in a resigned sort of way and shook his head slightly. Then he bowed to the court and simply sat down. I looked at the police prosecutor, expecting him to re-examine, but his eyes were on his papers. I looked at the magistrate, but he was busy writing his notes. The only person who was ready to look at me was the accused. He stared at me with an impassive face and bright mischievous eyes. For a second or two I simply stood there. Then the magistrate's head came up with a jerk. He seemed surprised to find me still there. He said, "Very well, Mr. Gilruth. Thank you very much. We shall not require any more of your time." He made the same small swallowing noise I had heard before. "Not today," he said. I looked at him and for what seemed quite a long time we looked at each

other with the bar of the court between us. He had
the power I had had twenty years before. It was no
concern of mine now what he did with it. All the
same, I stared into his small, uncommunicative eyes,
and presently he dropped them to his papers again.
I turned and stepped down from the box. A police
constable who probably understood no English
looked at me curiously, but everyone else seemed
busy elsewhere. I went slowly down to the back of
the court. I do not think the Subedar-Major saw me
until I came up to him and took his hand. His face
was rigid and grey, and his eyes stared behind his
thick glasses. He pressed my hand and said in a
harsh whisper, "You have given your evidence?"

"Yes," I said. "It is finished."

He looked up towards the bar of the court, but I
knew he could not see that far. He whispered again.
He said, "I cannot understand. I sent no telegram."

"I know," I said. "Someone sent it. It is not known
who."

He clenched his bony fist and beat it suddenly
and horribly against the side of his head. I thought,
"Not mad, not mad, sweet heaven." And then I
thought, why not? He could have little further use
for sanity. I did not know what else I could say to
him. But I saw that he had already forgotten that
I was there. He was staring up towards the invisible
fount of justice at the other end of the long room.
I left him and walked out into the sudden, dazzling

heat of the court compound. There were the usual clusters of people waiting. Perhaps more than usual, because the committal proceedings had been super-imposed on a program of work already fixed. I thought the police and the petition-writers looked at me with interest, as if they were in the know, but the rest simply waited. When their time came, they would be called. Until then there was nothing to do. I had nothing to wait for and there was nothing for me to do at all.

I walked slowly across the compound towards the road. The S.D.O.'s bungalow was there ahead of me, but I was not going there now, only to my borrowed car standing in the patchy shade of the acacias. I was going to drive it back to Rawalpindi. There tomorrow I should board a Trident jet with smart air-hostesses in fancy dress and fly down to Lahore and Karachi. I had made my booking as soon as the date of the committal proceedings had been fixed. By that time I had already known the answer. Nobody had suggested that I should make myself available to give evidence in the Sessions Court at Fazilpur. And today the magistrate had said that they would not need any more of my time. Then he had kecked and added, "Not today," but I knew what he meant. I knew from the smell of the court and the way he had dropped his eyes after telling me I could go. The case would not go to Sessions, any more than Bahadur's case had.

At Karachi there would be the sea, very flat and landlocked and unrecognizable, but the same sea, of one piece with all the other sea. That immortal sea that brought us hither. Only I had been brought through a trick of the time machine, by way of the characteristic lavatories of Frankfurt and Rome. So I took a last, hard look at Pind Fazl Shah, which clearly no longer existed, and which would never exist for me again once I was back in London. Then I got into my car. Even under the acacias the metal was almost too hot to touch. I remembered very clearly this feel and smell of a sun-baked car. In the old days the fuel pump used to lose its vacuum and stop working when it got too hot, and we had to swaddle it in damp rags to keep it cool and serviceable. But the old anxieties were out of date now, and my car was a Morris belonging, more or less, to the man I had just left in the courtroom over the road. It started perfectly, and I backed and turned it and headed for Rawalpindi.

The Nicholson memorial stood up in the white glare of the afternoon, and the rock ridges above it wavered and shimmered in the heat. It had the stubborn but imperfect evocativeness of a dream remembered in daylight. I reckoned it would cost quite a lot to shift, far more than a statue on the Mall. The clash between national pride and budgetary stringency might be a severe one. In any case, the dream was not my dream. I did not think it ever had been. My dream had always had an element of nightmare in it, and the daylight was not without its comfort. The cane wagons creaked and swayed on the road in their moving columns of dust. I saw them suddenly with a tourist's eye as picturesque components of a landscape with which I had no immediate contact. I had all night to catch my plane, and picked my way past them with leisurely discretion.

In the evening I went around the tourist shops to find a present for Estelle. A sort of holiday mood possessed me, an unreasonable lightness that insulated me from the unresolved conflicts of the immediate and remote past. I longed for the beautiful, astringent presence of a woman to whom India was just a job like any other job, and guilt an unfortunate disability you did not talk about, like constipation. I bought her an embroidered thing from Swat and a Baluchi garment sewn all over with little looking glasses, which she might perhaps wear for the fun of it on an evening at home. We had agreed not to write to each other. We had never been very long separated before, and I think we neither of us knew quite how to set about it. When I had booked my return flight, I had sent her a cable, but that was all.

Now I come to think about it, I fancy my mood that evening was not unlike my mood when I had left the country in 1947. There was at least the same underlying conviction that the time for casting up accounts was past, because whatever balance was struck could have no bearing on the future. The conviction was right, but I should have known, this time, that the mood which rested on it would not last. I carried Estelle's things back to the hotel and packed them on the top of my suitcase, where I could display them, for what they were worth, to the unemotional eye of the London customs. I did not think they would be worth much, but the thought of the smiling steely customs was as welcome in its way as the thought of the emotional inviolability of Estelle. I had walked too long on a shifting surface and longed for firmer going.

It was the hot weather now, only the beginning of it, but unmistakable. The world came out in clean clothes to stroll in the dusk. I dined early and went out strolling among them, as much a ghost as I had ever been, and wanting only to run myself down physically, so that I could be sure of sleeping when I made up my mind to do it. They had been watering the half-empty beds along the side of the Mall. The smell of the water on the hot dust was like a part of myself, so immediately familiar that I could not imagine myself ever being without it. Yet I knew that if once I gave it up and went into the hotel, I should never smell it again, and I kept on putting this off, because I was certain that the smell must be associated with something else, which

I had forgotten, but which I did not want to forgo.

In the end I knew that the association would not work. I still smelled the watered dust, but there was nothing more to come of it. I went back to the hotel. My suitcase was there, packed with Estelle's things on top and labeled for London. That was the only thing that was going to happen to me now. The smell of watered dust had no relevance at all.

CHAPTER

19

I HEARD SOMEONE MOVING IN THE SITTING ROOM BE-
yond the curtained doorway. I did not know how
long I had been asleep. Not very long, because I had
been awake a long time after I got to bed. I sat up,
remembering that I had not put the hook across the
wire doors on to the verandah. It was not fully dark,
though there was no suggestion of daylight. When
the curtains parted, I saw at once who it was. I held
out my arms to her. She came and sat on the edge of
the bed, and we clung to each other without saying
a word. Then she said in my ear, "You ought to lock
your door. It isn't safe."

I said, "Damn safety."

She whispered again. "I only got back this evening. Patrick's still away. I phoned the hotel. They
told me you were going tomorrow morning. I tried
to phone you twice after dinner, but you weren't

here. I didn't want to phone again. You have to go through the hotel switchboard. At first I meant to give it up. Then I couldn't sleep, so I got up and came round. I mustn't stay long. Tell me what happened."

I told her, in quick short sentences, with my mouth against her ear. She shook her head, and her fingers tightened on me. She said, "I'm so sorry, I'm so sorry," apologizing for unrequited murder as she had apologized for the hotel food the first time I had met her.

I said, "I started it," and she said, "No, no," and put her fingers up as if to close my mouth. I kissed them. "No, listen," she said, "you didn't start anything. I told you. It was the custom of the country long before you got here."

"Then it was my job to end it. What was my job if it wasn't that?"

She said, "You shouldn't have come back."

"I think I had to," I said. "At any rate, I'm glad I did."

She swiveled away from me and stared into my face in the faint glimmer from the skylights. "You really are?" she said.

"Yes," I said. "Not only because of you."

"Why, then, apart from me?"

"I'm not quite sure. I told you, I shall know more when I get home. But I think I've salvaged something from what had been total loss."

"Then I'm glad," she said. She got up and stood by the side of the bed, holding my hands in hers. She said, "Shall I go now?"

"Not yet."

"All right. But soon."

"Soon, then," I said, "but not yet."

It was still dark outside when we went out into the verandah. The smell of watered dust was still in the air, but now the thing was complete. I did not sleep the rest of the night, but lay there, waiting to go home. At Lahore I saw nothing but the airport. At Karachi, although it was daylight and a long way off, I smelled the sea, just as I had smelled the country when I first got there. The sea I smelled was still that immortal sea of twenty years ago, which only the soul could have sight of. I myself, next morning, went up the gangway into a B.O.A.C. VC-10, and from then on had to deal with the things in front of my eyes.

Apart from the exotic landscapes below, the plane was as near being London as made no difference. It was like watching a travel film in a West End cinema. We had our foreign element, but they were visitors, expected to understand English and act as far as possible British. The cabin crew saw to their conformity with the kindly intolerance of Metropolitan policemen. I had only to sit and wait, and London itself would envelop me, for better or worse, in the consciousness of the person I now was.

238

Meanwhile, like the dying nerve of a worn-out tooth, my old self nagged at me to be conscious of its trouble underneath. But there was nothing I could do about it, except let it die. There was nothing I could do for anyone in the world I had left, no possible act of reconciliation that would admit the ultimate possibility of innocence. The only thing to do was to sit and wait. We should soon be in London.

We got to London late on a bright and breezy afternoon. Even in this world of tarmac and concrete the few green things looked unbelievably green. The world itself was a sharp, clean world, still, for all its troubles, resting on a substratum of hard thought and careful organization. I remembered as a fact that when I had come home in 1947, I had delighted even in the London suburbs, because they were so orderly and so indefeasibly English. This remembered delight had since become unintelligible, but now, for an hour or so, I understood it again. When all was said and done, what I had wanted, in the days of my innocence, was to make Pind Fazl Shah, at least in some ways, more like Twickenham. My failure was understandable, but the intention had not been wholly unreasonable or wholly wrong.

The airport bus ran out into the fast-moving traffic, and at the terminal I was no longer a traveler, but merely a Londoner with hand baggage, looking for a taxi to take him home. Estelle would be at home by now, shaking out her hair in front of her glass, but I was going to my own flat first. I was going to unpack and wash and change, all with conscious deliberation, and then go around to her as much as possible as if I had not been away more than an unavoidable day or two.

I had headed off any correspondence that mattered, and I had no great interest in the scatter of envelopes that I stepped over when I opened the door. The flat was musty and deadly quiet, but I was pleased to see it again. I put my things down and went around opening windows and running taps. It was only then that I gathered up the post. I found a letter from Estelle face down on top of it. It was heavy. There was an immediate stab of disappointment, because the mere existence of the letter meant that I was not going to see her that evening. When I opened the envelope and found the keys of her flat inside, bundled up in a separate sheet of paper, I still told myself that she was away and had left me the keys in case I wanted anything of mine from her flat. I read the letter standing there between my pieces of baggage, with the useless post clutched in a bundle in my left hand. I sat down in my usual chair and read it through again, forcing myself this time to read it carefully and in detail. Although we did not write to each other, Estelle wrote a very competent letter.

Then I refolded the letter, put it on the arm of my chair and sat back with my eyes shut. I had always known that this would happen some time. I had never thought of Toby Cooper, but that was mainly a professional complication. What I had not faced was the extent of my dependence. The question was how I was going to go on at all, as things were at this moment, on my own. The letter was completely final. I was the only person left in the calculation, and it was a calculation I did not seem very well qualified to make. My old self was irremediably lost to me, and now my present self had lost, at a blow, nearly all its defenses. I did not see what there was to go on with, though I accepted it as a matter of course that something would go on. Ultimately there was a book to be written. I knew it had to be written, but I also knew what writing it would be like, and I recoiled from the thought as I recoiled from the thought of unanesthetized surgery. That was the only thing to do, but I did not think I could do it yet.

I opened my suitcase and took out the things I had bought for Estelle. I put them carefully in an empty drawer at the bottom of my clothes cupboard. The Baluchi thing was really very charming. I supposed someone would like it some time. I shut the drawer firmly and then, as the next thing to be done, went on with my unpacking.

>>> If you've enjoyed this book and would like to discover more great vintage crime and thriller titles, as well as the most exciting crime and thriller authors writing today, visit: **>>>**

The Murder Room
Where Criminal Minds Meet

themurderroom.com

9 781471 900631